Sandspun

Sandspun

Annette J. Bruce
J. Stephen Brooks

Pineapple Press, Inc.
Sarasota, Florida

Inquiries should be addressed to:

Pineapple Press, Inc.
P.O. Box 3889
Sarasota, Florida 34230
www.pineapplepress.com

Library of Congress Cataloging-in-Publication Data

Sandspun / [compiled by] Annette J. Bruce, J. Stephen Brooks.
      p. cm.
   Includes indexes.
    ISBN 1-56164-242-8 (hardbound : alk. paper) – ISBN 1-56164-243-6 (pbk. : alk. paper)
1. Short stories, American—Florida. 2. Florida—Social life and customs—Fiction. I. Bruce, Annette J. II. Brooks, J. Stephen

PS558.F6 S26 2001
813'.010832759—dc21   2001023496

First Edition
10 9 8 7 6 5 4 3 2 1

Design by Shé Sicks
Printed in the United States of America

Table of Contents

Central Florida: The Ridge and West Coast   51

South Florida   95

Dedications

This book is dedicated to the memory of

Thelma Ann Boltin
(1904–1992)

She Celebrated Life

Thelma Ann Boltin, affectionately known as Cousin Thelma to the thousands who attended the annual Florida Folk Festival held at the Stephen Foster Folk Culture Center in White Springs, was a folk singer, lecturer, taleteller, emcee, writer, and collector of folklore. Thelma referred to the audience as her "kissin' cousins," and they came up to her and introduced themselves as her cousins from Miami, Atlanta, or Jacksonville who had not missed a festival since 1953. Thus began a legend among folk enthusiasts in the Southeast.

Cousin Thelma was born in Beaufort, South Carolina, on August 31, 1904, but she was quick to say that she considered herself to be a Floridian as she had celebrated her third birthday in Gainesville, Florida. Her father, William Golden Boltin, established a thriving Coca-Cola bottling company in Gainesville. Although he was a successful, busy businessman, he found the time and energy every night to tell stories around the supper table.

Thelma was educated in the Alachua County public schools as well as in her home and in Miss Maggie Teabeau's School for Young Women. She laughingly told me that while in school, being redheaded, freckled, four-eyed (she wore glasses), and overweight was enough to give her a lifelong complex. But she still took part in many high school stage productions and convinced her mother to persuade her father to let her go north to attend Emerson College in Boston, which offered an excellent program in drama. Yes, she aspired to be on Broadway and the silver screen. Can you imagine the culture shock she must have experienced when she arrived in Boston?

She regaled me with how her speech teachers had to work overtime to make her shed her Southern drawl. She received her degree in English, Dramatics, and Speech, with a particular focus on folklore and folk dancing. She returned to Florida and became the first certified full-time speech teacher in the state. During the war years, she came out of the classroom and headed up the servicemen and servicewomen's center (USO) in Gainesville.

Ms. Boltin was a participant in the first and second Florida Folk Festivals as a storyteller. She told about her family's ghost, "Old Knocker," who lived in a large upright glass cabinet. In early festivals, she played the autoharp and sang, but she always told at least one tale from her vast repertoire of Uncle Remus and Boltin Family stories.

In 1954, Thelma was asked to direct the Florida Folk Festival. Although Cousin Thelma never owned a car, she traveled up and down the state, scouting out talent, promoting the Florida Folk Festival and other special events at the center, and presenting her program, entitled "Florida Lore in Song and Story." During the Florida Folk Festival's infancy, no participants were paid. Many a performer came solely because of his or her great admiration for the Florida Folk Festival, Stephen Foster Memorial, Cousin Thelma, and the work of the staff. A newsletter was sent out twice a year to keep performers up to date on happenings in the folk community. It contained information on who would be attending the next folk festival and tidbits about folk performers. Thus, a Florida Folk Festival Family was born with Cousin Thelma reigning as the matriarch.

She had a collection of witty sayings she relied on when needed, such as, "The old cow's tail hangs down behind. It may be ugly and full of cockleburs, but the old cow loves it, 'cause it's hers!" These lines were followed by a big guffaw, never failing to bring peals of laughter from the audience. She would begin each festival with, "One for the money, two for the show, three to make ready, and four to go!" And closed it with, "See you next year, cousins."

Because of her dramatic training, Cousin Thelma was accused of always being "on stage." But I learned over the years that this was just her way. It won her many a friend. Thelma Ann Boltin, a Florida folk figure, died on December 5, 1992, but her legend lives on—continued by the hundreds of "cousins" (count me as one) who commemorate her by recalling her way of telling a story, her zest for cooking and eating, her laughter, and the many other ways she celebrated life.

—Barbara Beauchamp

Barbara Beauchamp was Thelma Boltin's coworker, driver, and friend. Barbara was a participant in the first Florida Folk Festival and helped lead the festival to national prominence. She has dedicated more than forty years to the documentation, presentation, and preservation of the traditional culture of Florida. Barbara is still "a mover and a shaker." She was one of the 1999 recipients of the Florida Folk Heritage Awards—a deserving tribute.

And to the memory of

Will McLean
(1919–1990)

Florida's Black Hat Troubadour

Will McLean was born near Chipley, Florida. His love of music was nurtured by his grandfather, who gave him his first instrument, a gourd-and-cornstalk fiddle with a horsehair bow. McLean's love of Florida developed as he traveled the state from the Panhandle hardwood hammocks to the vast Everglades—camping in wilderness areas, visiting friends, and absorbing Florida history.

Though he found time to appear at concerts, festivals, schools, and even Carnegie Hall, Will McLean is best known as the "Father of Florida Folk." In 1996, he was honored with induction into the Florida Artists Hall of Fame, the first folk artist to be so recognized.

One of the most colorful aspects of Will's performances was the way he would "bring on" his songs. Indeed, these song introductions often took on the characteristics of epic narratives. With much fanfare and hyperbole, Will would extol his heroes from Florida's past. He would speak of the great, the near great, the obscure, and the absurd with an equal measure of heroic reverence. Will was not one to underestimate his own contribution to Florida history and folk art. When he performed his songs and stories, we were not only entertained, we were educated. We were being invited to share in Will's own heroic vision of Florida and the characters who walked upon his Florida sand. Will's best-known songs include "Hold Back the Waters," "Osceola's Last Words," "Wild Hog," "Ballad of Silver Springs," and "Away O'ee" (written at the age of six).

Will was well known in the folk and storytelling communities for showing up to visit—maybe for an hour or maybe a week. He would pick and sing story songs about Florida or swap stories about events he'd seen or been part of. Before you knew it, you were there. He held the attention of his audiences just by being himself, which is all he ever wanted to be. He was happiest camped out in the woods somewhere in his beloved Florida. He seemed to always have a comical comment to cheer all of us who knew him.

Cancer claimed Will's life in January 1990. Gore's Landing was one of his favorite places and that is where his ashes were scattered to the wind and water. Today, his spirit soars like a hawk over his beloved Florida sand.

—J. Stephen Brooks

My Soul Is a Hawk

My soul is a hawk . . . I am but returned from the place the Indians call: "Land where the Wind is born."
Into the quiet and lonely spaces of the upper skies soar I.
The beauty of Florida below me
As thermal air currents send their song thru my wing-feathers,
And I float in ever-widening circles—yellow eyes piercing in rapture.
The blues and golds, the orange and faint-pinks of sunset,
And I see in the far-far distance . . . my haven—the majes-tic-old-dead tree
On whose limbs I find . . .
My soul is a hawk.

From "My Soul Is a Hawk" by Will McLean. Used by permission of Margaret Longhill.

And to the memory of

J. Gamble Rogers
(1938–1991)

An extraordinary guitar picker, storyteller, and friend to mankind

Gamble Rogers and Will McLean were among my best friends when I moved to St. Augustine in February 1967. It was our music, of course, that bound us together. To counterbalance the insanity of playing all those juke joints and bars, we would hitch up Gamble's old Thompson's Runabout to his split-pea soup–green Mustang and haul that boat over to the Oklawaha River.

Gamble was always the captain of the ship, and he always perceived irony in everything he saw. Will comfortably sprawled midships, telling endless stories about Florida. I would crawl out on the bow with my old Leica M 2 and photograph wildflowers, birds, and riverviews, the likes of which my eyes had never before seen.

Gamble became a lifelong friend and picking pal. In many ways he was the brother I never had. We could talk to each other about things that we could not talk about to others. Gamble went on to develop his own stories about Florida. No surprise to me that they took place in Oklawaha County. Those wonderful characters he created were people just like you and me caught up in life's little ironies.

These men are gone now. My love for Florida was fostered by my relationship with these friends. Because of them, Florida is now, and will always be, a place in my heart.

—Bob Patterson

Taken from the title insert of the CD A Place in My Heart *by Bob Patterson. Used by permission.*

Overheard at the 1999 Gamble Rogers Folk Festival: "I'm yet to meet the person who knew Gamble Rogers that does not say, 'He was my friend.'"

Gamble Rogers always had a smile and a warm welcome. I was always amazed at his wonderful facility for language and his ability to talk to his audience—maybe while setting up his story and at the same time picking out a classical guitar melody softly in the background. I guess "effortless" would describe him, because whether performing or just greeting his legions of fans, he had an effortless way of making you feel welcome.

He Was My Kind Of Man!

I remember Gamble Rogers being personable,
And he was, in Jay Smith's words, "very approachable."
A man of youthful ideas and vitality,
Who masterly blended fantasy with reality.
I remember Gamble Rogers! Oh yes, that I can,
And say without hesitation, "He was my kind of man!"

I remember G.R. making friends by being one.
A gifted man of many words, he crafted for fun.
A talented musician with many a devotee,
Yet, a gentle but strong man—proud of his family.
I remember Gamble Rogers! Oh yes, that I can,
And say without hesitation, "He was my kind of man!"

It was not for a loved-one, but a complete stranger,
That G. R. proved his mettle by battling danger.
Florida will long mourn the death of her beloved son,
Gamble Rogers, the courageous, apt, and caring one.
I remember Gamble Rogers! Oh yes, that I can!
And say without hesitation, "He was my kind of man!"

He was my kind of man—making his guitar chuckle and moan.
He was my kind of man—making tales of Bean Creek his own.
He was my kind of man—facing eternity, unafraid.
He was my kind of man—his life was sterling with gold overlaid.

—Annette J. Bruce

Acknowledgments

We wish to express our gratitude to everyone who contributed to the successful completion of this book. Anne Blackshear, Rita Chaney, Mary Fears, Tyler Fisher, Helen Floyd, Jamye Green, Don Leonard, Nadyne McGladdery, Barbara McIntyre, John McLaughlin, Ann Mancebo, and Roy Moye made contributions, as did Peggy Perrin, Frances Rinaldi, Jane Sims, Rick Stone, and Lila Watson. It is our wish that you keep on telling and keep on writing. We want to hear you tell and to see your stories in print.

A special expression of gratitude is due Wilton and Diane Rooks for saving the manuscript from extinction in the innards of the PC monster.

We would also like to acknowledge the tremendous amount of work done by David and June Cussen and their entire staff at Pineapple Press. Every Florida citizen and visitor is indebted to the folks at Pineapple Press for their commitment to seek out and publish manuscripts with Florida themes that are not only helpful but entertaining.

Thank you!

—J. Stephen Brooks and Annette Bruce

Preface

As an educator for the past forty years and trained well beyond my intelligence, I have come to realize that much of my job is not simply to pass along others' wisdom. It is to help folks create some of their own to go with those universal truths we all try to live by. How one goes about accomplishing that is the art form of education.

We've all heard it said, "If you really want to get to know something, you just better go there and spend some time root'n' about." That gem is still one of the best pieces of advice anyone could offer another. However, in the application of that principle, one discovers that it just isn't possible. Cost, red tape, transportation, time constraints, resistance, and other problems stop that journey in its tracks. No problem! As an educator, I would simply go to plan B and suggest, "OK, just sit down and listen to their stories." Listening to stories that are well crafted and well told allows others to have a visit in the setting of that story.

Though we all find ourselves trapped within an electronic communication era, stories continue to be as important for people of today as they were for past cultures. They've existed to inform us how to live out our lives. They allow us to learn from others and through their ways. They offer us benchmarks for quality living. Stories serve as the vehicle for communicating the beliefs, knowledge, religions, ethics, laws, humor, and values of all people. Story is a natural and universal container for collecting and crafting information and imagination so it may be saved, shared, and remembered. Story is significant in itself for it exists only because an individual felt that something was so important that it must be saved and passed along to others.

Storytellers are the means by which stories and their wisdom may be revealed. As stories are shared, folks learn to listen with a different point of view. They recognize the wisdom of the stories and sense the awe and joy of the experience when transcending into other dimensions of now and here. They discover that it is not the teller but rather the story that teaches. They understand that they must be open and receptive to receive the gift of stories. That's true because the act of telling is unconditional in nature, and people learn through that experience to trust the ways of the storyteller and his stories. This is true for teachers, leaders, neighbors, parents, and children. Storytelling empowers stewards of family, community, and culture to help craft, share, and celebrate the wonder of life.

Storytelling creates a place and time where honor, reverence, delight, and trust serve as the ways for carrying out our daily activities. People listen to stories because they are interesting, meaningful, and entertaining. Following a storytelling experience within a fifth-grade classroom, a student sent me a thank-you note. He said, "I wasn't having a good day until you came in and told your stories. I thought you came to teach us something. You really did, but not by talking to us . . . by telling a story!" I love that!

Stories may be shared at the dinner table, school, concert hall, place of work, or any location. When it occurs, it creates a shared-energy knowledge that is felt and understood by those who were present. That is why a story must be told and shared time and again!

A community is bound together as its truth is shared through story. That art form of life events, storytelling, will continue to broaden and enrich one's life and culture when enacted by teller and listener, for story does not simply describe life—it creates life in its sharing.

Annette J. Bruce and J. Stephen Brooks have embarked upon that mission with their most recent collection of Florida tales by Florida tellers. It is a generous gift of Florida tales put to print in an authentic, humorous, and artful manner. They have spun a collection of tales—whether fable, fact, or yarn—that walk the trails of Florida with flair and understanding of where you live.

—Dr. Jim Mittelstadt, College of Education and Human Services, University of North Florida

Introduction

This collection was initially inspired by a young man whose life was passing before his eyes as a gator gained on him . . . okay, I'll admit, that's a tall tale. But as one who has been a Florida boy since elementary school, and one who loved hearing the tales of Florida while growing up, and one who became a man who told tales, I believe the stories in this collection represent some of the alluring lore that's made Florida such a draw to the rest of the world.

From the north come tales such as "The Devil's Millhopper," and "Snitch and Snatch." Some are true, some are suspect, but all are delightful.

Then we drift down to the central region of Florida, with tales of pirates such as "Gaspar," "Man's Best Friend," and "Monkey the Trickster," tongue-in-cheek and fantastical—similar to modern-day central Florida.

Next, we drift to tellers who live in the beach region, or at least a part of it. Both Daytona and the Cape Canaveral area enjoy worldwide recognition, and the tellers there have provided us with more stories designed to bring a chuckle, such as "Cousin Cassie's Cooking," and those designed to cause goose bumps, like "Kissimmee Bound."

Finally, we get to the lower half of the state, which has its own character. Ghosts, outlandish characters, and animals are all represented by the tellers from this region of Florida, just as it has been since the region was first discovered and settled. After all, Florida's flora and fauna inspire stories, and those stories inspire settlers, who then tell more stories . . . and the cycle goes on *ad infinitum*.

As one who has soaked up the lore of Florida for over forty years, I can attest to the fact that you'll enjoy these collected tales. So sit back and enjoy.

—J. Stephen Brooks

Growing up in Florida, the stories I read were not only "once upon a time," but also "once upon a place"—some far-off place. But my story-telling father added that special touch to his stories by placing them in familiar settings. I felt that his stories were homespun (maybe I should say "sandspun") and the stories in print were store bought. I remember the thrill when I read my first book set in Florida. I think the title of the book was *Orange Winter*. It has long been out of print, and the local library lost its only copy a number of years ago. I do not recall the author's name, but the lessons in ecology, which were an underlying theme in the book, are still fresh in my mind.

The stories in this collection reflect the flora and fauna of Florida, but because they are stories written and told by storytellers, many of them, like my father's, are old folktales that have been recast and placed in Florida settings. Some are personal stories and a few are original stories baited with historical nuggets. Each one was selected with your pleasure in mind.

Folktales are the easiest stories to tell—they are always recommended for beginning storytellers. They may have never been true, but they have truth in them. Told with enough human interest and humor, they will be preserved for many years and even more listeners. Because of the dearth of storytelling in the home, children especially enjoy the personal stories. And the action-packed story with a few historical facts is the favorite genre of the thousands of newcomers who every month make Florida their home.

Florida was the scene of the most romantic quests of all time—the search for the Fountain of Youth, as well as the long-fought wars with the Seminoles. Its history is pregnant with romantic figures whose struggles for personal and religious freedom were so dramatic that we tend to lose sight of the bigotry, selfishness, politics, and other sordid factors of those turbulent days. Much of human history must be reconstructed from skimpy records, but Floridians have a rich heritage, and rich rewards await all the readers, tellers, and listeners of stories of Florida's colorful past.

The book is divided geographically so that each contributor's stories appear together with their author's picture and his or her brief biography. In order to keep these sections about the same size, central Florida was divided into two: the East Coast and the Ridge and West Coast. A topical index is included in the back.

Although the only requirement for submitting a story for consideration was that the story have a Florida connection, most of the manuscripts were submitted by members of the Florida Storytelling Association. Most of the serious storytellers in Florida are members, and the association was the best means of getting the word out to would-be contributors. We did have a few offerings from non-members.

Many tellers tell stories (with permission) that are under someone else's copyright and could not submit them for print. The stories we included are the ones chosen by the publisher and editors from the submissions as the cream of the crop. Enjoy!

—Annette J. Bruce

North Florida

The north section of Florida was settled first and is the only part of the state to have ever had a plantation economy, reportedly creating a unique folk culture and producing many tale-tellers. Maybe these tellers, even more so than those elsewhere in the state, agreed with Richard Chase when he wrote, "It is only when our old songs and old tales are passing from one human being to another, by word-of-mouth, that they can attain their full fascination. No printed page can create this spell. It is the living word—the sung ballad and the told tale—that holds our attention and reaches our hearts."

This collection was greatly enhanced by the contributions of these north Florida tellers: Nancy Case, Elaine Kitchings, Bob Patterson, and Diane Rooks. Each story gives the reader a glimpse of one of Florida's colorful landscapes. Enjoy!

—Annette J. Bruce

"A story, once heard, becomes a part of you. The humor, the magic, and the mystery of stories told around campfires and at family gatherings have been part of my life since childhood. I hope that my tales will become part of your life."

Nancy L. Case
Gainesville

Although her parents lived in Greenville, Florida, Nancy Case was born in Thomasville, Georgia, because the closest hospital was located there. Nancy is a fifth-generation Floridian.

Nancy received her master's degree in Educational Media from the University of South Florida and for nearly twenty years was employed as a media specialist in both Pasco and Alachua County schools. Since 1999, Nancy has been Media Supervisor for Alachua County schools. Nancy has been telling stories professionally for more than fifteen years. She is a frequent teller at festivals throughout the state and can also be heard spinning her tales in libraries, schools, bookstores, and other venues. She has taught classes in storytelling for the Santa Fe Community Education Program. In March 2001, she became president of the Florida Storytelling Association. She is one of the founders—and for many years served as the chairperson—of the Alachua County Schools Storytelling Festival. Nancy is the creator of *Tales of Granny Fanny* and author of *Rooster Tales.*

Nancy has been married to husband Ronald for over thirty years. They have two grown daughters.

The Devil's Millhopper

The Devil's Millhopper is a geological formation near Gainesville, Florida. It is actually a large sinkhole, its sides covered with many rocks and lush vegetation. The Millhopper began to form nearly ten thousand years ago and reached its present form about nine thousand years later. The sinkhole measures over 500 feet across and 120 feet deep. At the bottom there is a small pool, which is fed by tiny springs in the rocky walls of the sinkhole.

The Millhopper is a beautiful place that has been enjoyed by thousands of visitors over the years as a favorite scenic spot and picnic area. The site was once used as a natural amphitheater. In my father's college days, during University of Florida fraternity hazing, he was blindfolded, taken to the Millhopper in the dead of night, and thrown off the side, only to be caught by a large net near the bottom.

Today the Florida Park Service administers the site, and visitors may climb down steep wooden stairways to the bottom of the sinkhole. Any ancient geological formation is likely to have many folktales passed on about its origin. The Devil's Millhopper is no exception. This is my version of one of my favorite legends about the Millhopper.

Far back in the mists of time, long before the Seminoles came, there were ancient Indian nations living in the northeast portion of what later became known as Florida. In the area we now know as Alachua County, there was once a certain tribe of Indians inhabiting the land. Among this nation was a beautiful Indian maiden called Little Flower. Her hair was as sleek and black as the crow's wing. Her eyes were brown as a doe's and her feet were quick in the dance. She was kind and loving in every way. All the people of the tribe loved her, and every young girl wished to be as beautiful as she.

All the young braves of the tribe tried to win her affection but to no avail, for the beautiful young maiden loved a handsome Indian brave called Running Fox, and he loved her as well. Running Fox was tall and brave, and the two of them planned to be married at the next full moon.

One day the Devil took the form of a man and was walking in the forest nearby. As he approached a small stream, he saw the beautiful maiden filling a jug with water. She leaned over the water to see her reflection, and her shiny black hair fell over her shoulder like a waterfall. The Devil could see she was no ordinary girl. She was more beautiful than any flower in the forest. That moment he decided that she must be his bride.

To induce her to marry him, the Devil took the form of a handsome Indian brave and approached the stream where Little Flower was standing. He did his best to woo her, but she explained that she was in love with and promised to another. The Devil refused to take no for an answer and continued to try to entice her. He boasted about what a great hunter he was and promised that she would never be hungry if she agreed to marry him. Again, the beautiful maiden explained that she could never love him and would never be his wife.

Still the Devil coaxed and bartered. He offered her many beautiful things. In fact, he promised her anything she might want if only she would love him forever and be his wife. The kindly maiden consoled him as best she could, and again she told him that beautiful things could not change her heart for it was already given to Running Fox.

In a rage, the Devil left and returned to his home in the underworld, but he didn't forget the beautiful young woman. Each day he wanted her more than the day before, and all his thoughts were of revenge. Finally his decision was made—he would take her from the earth and force her to marry him whether she wished to or not!

One day, not long before Little Flower and Running Fox were to be married, the Devil came to earth again. In the dark of the night, he stole the beautiful maiden away but not before Running Fox heard her screams. Running Fox called for help and ran swiftly after the pair. The Devil ran quickly but the weight of the young woman in his arms slowed him down. Soon the young brave was about to overtake them.

Realizing that at any moment Running Fox might catch up with them, the Devil stopped abruptly and stamped his foot on the ground three times. The earth began to shake and tremble. There was a loud rumble, and a great hole shaped like a hopper or funnel formed in the

Sandspun

earth leading down to the underworld. The Devil took Little Flower down into the deep hole, and there they disappeared from view, never to be seen again. In a few moments the entrance to the underworld sealed itself behind them. Only the echo of the demon's evil laugh and the great pit remained.

The heartbroken brave and the other tribal members who had followed him knelt on the sides of the pit to weep for Little Flower. As their tears flowed to the bottom of the pit and formed a small pool, the Devil exacted his final revenge and, with a snap of his fingers, transformed them all into stone.

If you visit the Devil's Millhopper near Gainesville, you can see that those stones continue to weep to this day. Little Flower has not been forgotten. Her people still weep for her return.

© 1995 Nancy L. Case
storylady1@hotmail.com

For another version of this legend and other legends about the Devil's Millhopper, see First Citizens and Other Florida Folks: Essays on Florida Folklife, *edited by Ronald Foreman, published by the Bureau of Florida Folklife Programs, Division of Archives, History, and Records Management, 1984.*

"I found my niche as a children's librarian and developed a deep love in sharing my stories with children and adults. Oftentimes, in my audiences you'll find my husband, Earl, our son, William Earl Sr., and our daughter-in-law, Angela, with our two grandsons, Cemal and William Earl Jr. What joy!"

Elaine Fears Kitchings
Jacksonville

In the early 1930s, Ernest and Juanita Fears decided that Tallahassee, Florida, would be the ideal place to rear their one son and two daughters because of the college that was located there. So, leaving Leesburg, Florida, they moved to the capital city. Elaine graduated from Florida A & M University and received her MLS from Atlanta University. She was employed with the Jacksonville Public Library for thirty-two years, retiring from the Bradham Brooks Northwest Branch. Membership in the Florida Storytelling Association, National Storytelling Network, and National Storytellers League has enabled her to strengthen her skills as a storyteller. Elaine has served several terms on the board of directors for the Florida Storytelling Association, and she and Yvette Thomas are cofounders of the Northside Storytellers League.

Angelina and Cigam

In the time of long ago, along the bank of the Suwannee River in a small cabin lived Angelina and her mama. Warning her every day not to go into the swamps, Angelina's mama would say, "Now, Angelina, don't you go into the dark woods of the swamps, and whatever you do, don't talk to a strange-looking little man carrying a shiny orange rock in his hands. He can charm you right into the woods with that rock. Why, some folk say he can make you smaller than the leg of a flea. Folk even say this man is a man of magic. Now, Babycake, you know your mama don't want nothin' to happen to you."

"Don't you worry 'bout me, Mama-lamb, for I'm gonna surely be lookin' out for this little man all the time. I don't wanna be changed into nothin'," she said as she skipped 'round the big basket of clothes her mama filled from the clothesline.

One day, playing near the edge of the deep, dark woods, Angelina saw a strange-looking flower just inside the woods. It glowed bright orange, and she reached for it. But each time she reached, the flower moved farther into the woods. After a while, Angelina looked around and the deep, dark woods of the swamp surrounded her. She turned to leave, but there in front of her stood the strangest-looking little man she had ever seen. In his hands was a shiny orange rock. Angelina looked at it, and it glowed so brightly.

The little man, wearing glittering red boots with turned-up toes, a tall pointed blue hat, breeches of purple, and a coat of green, had a wicked smile upon his face. His eyes were squinty; his nose was long and pointed with a large wart on its tip. His hair and beard were stringy and gray. He rubbed the glowing rock. Angelina feared that this was the man of magic. The little man beckoned her to come closer and she did, never taking her eyes from the glowing orange rock.

"Who are you?" she asked softly.

"I call myself Cigam. I have lived in these woods along this river-bank for many years. Some riddles I'll ask you—some short, some tall. Each time you cannot answer, I'll make you small. Five riddles unanswered will keep you in the woods with me. Answer all five and I'll set you free."

What will Mama think if I'm not home in time for supper? thought Angelina, and she began to cry.

Cigam asked the first riddle as he rubbed the glowing orange rock. "There is a house with neither windows nor doors, yet it holds two liquids with colors unmixed. What is it?"

Angelina sat down on the floor of the deep, dark woods trying to think of an answer. "I don't know what that is," she said softly. "Ask me another one."

Cigam snapped his fingers, and Angelina became one size smaller. She never even noticed the change. Cigam delighted in seeing his magic work.

Rubbing his rock again, he said, "Riddle number two. I have four legs and one foot and I cannot walk. I have a head and I cannot talk. What am I?"

Looking around as if to find an answer, Angelina said, "Surely hope I'll have some answers to these riddles before it's too late, but nothing is coming into my mind. I'll try to answer the next one."

"You're taking too long," shouted Cigam. "Just for that, I'm gonna make you two sizes smaller each time." Snapping his fingers, she became two sizes smaller. Pulling his gray, stringy beard, he began to think about his third riddle. A smirky grin came over his face as he watched his magic work. "Look down at yourself, and see how small you are becoming," Cigam said to Angelina.

Looking at her hands and feet, she could not believe how small she had become. The glowing orange rock was brighter than ever.

Cigam asked his third riddle. "What has teeth but cannot bite nor eat?"

After a few moments, Angelina cried out, "Please don't ask me any more riddles. Look what you are doing to me. I don't know the answers to your silly riddles."

Snap! Snap! She was two sizes smaller. Spinning on his heels and turning cartwheels all over the place, Cigam was a happy little man. "My magic is working," he shouted as loudly as he could. Dancing around Angelina, he said, "Riddle number four, the easiest of them all.

Where will the cat be when the lights go out?"

"I don't know. I don't know!" cried Angelina. "Please don't make me any smaller." Cigam placed the orange rock in front of the pill-sized Angelina and continued to dance around her. He clicked his heels and snapped his fingers. The more he danced, the more the orange rock glowed. Suddenly, the orange rock began to flash—on, off, on, off.

"This is the big one," shouted Cigam. "Listen! Backwards! Backwards! Once or twice. Tell me my true name or pay the price. It starts with M and ends with C. Five letters are there, so spell it with care. Answer all five riddles and you will see—back in your cabin in your bed you will be."

Angelina was now smaller than Cigam's little finger. He began to dance so fast around Angelina, it made her head spin. She soon fell into a deep sleep.

Crying aloud the answers to his riddles, though asleep, she said, "An egg is a house holding unmixed colors."

Would you believe she grew a size taller? Cigam watched and heard it all. He could not believe this.

He heard her say again, "A bed has a head, four legs, and one foot. A bed cannot talk nor walk." Again, she grew two sizes taller.

Stirring in her sleep, she murmured the next answer, "A comb has teeth but cannot bite nor eat."

Snap! Snap! She was two sizes taller. Pulling his hat quickly from his head and jumping up and down upon it, Cigam said with fright, "My magic! My magic! What is happening to my magic?"

Then he heard her say, "A cat will be in the dark when the lights go out."

Cigam saw a smile come onto her face. He was furious. Leaning over her, he whispered, "You still have not answered the big one. You will never guess my name. Backwards! Backwards! Once or twice. Tell me my true name or pay the price."

Quickly awakening from her sleep, she sat up and said, "It's Magic! Cigam is Magic spelled backwards!"

Looking down at her hands and feet, she said, "I'm back to my size again."

Angelina looked all around her. She was back in her own cabin, in her own little room, and there beside her bed was her own sweet Mama-lamb.

"Oh, you're awake, Babycake," said her mama. "You've been having a bad dream and shouting words I don't understand."

Angelina looked up at her mama with the biggest smile on her face and said, "Mama, let me tell you about this little man I saw in the deep, dark woods." And so she did.

Angelina's mama grabbed her and gave her a great big hug and said, "Lawd, Babycake, you nearly scared me to death." She reached out to take Angelina's hand and noticed it was tightly closed. "Angelina, what's in your hand?"

Angelina looked down at her hand and slowly uncurled each finger. To her surprise, nestled in the palm of her tiny, dirt-smudged hand was a bright, shiny orange rock.

© Elaine Fears Kitchings

A Strong Woman

The true story of a strong woman, Mrs. Mary McLeod Bethune

The year is 1899. Travel with me to the small, Southern town of Palatka on the St. Johns River in Florida. Meet Mary, a large woman of dark skin—a black woman who has a burning desire to build a school and educate black girls.

Mary Bethune, her husband, and their son, Albert, came from South Carolina to Palatka, where she wanted to build her school. But each time she attempted to build, someone burned it down. Some believed it was the work of the Ku Klux Klan, but there was never any proof. The stress was too much for her husband, and he no longer wanted to share her dream, so they separated.

In 1904, Mrs. Bethune learned that the Florida East Coast Railroad was building a railroad in Daytona. She knew that if a railroad was being built, they would be using black laborers and these laborers would have children who needed an education.

Taking her son, Albert, by the hand, she boarded the train. This train would take them over the St. Johns River and down the Atlantic Coast to Daytona. She sat in the section of the train reserved for blacks, which was required by the law that reinforced segregation. But this did not bother Mary. She must have felt as though she was riding the freedom train.

Resting her head against the back of her seat and patting the shoulder of her small son, she began to remember. She recalled her mother and father, Patsy and Samuel McLeod, and how they had told her they did not know how to read or write because they were children of slaves. She remembered how, as a child, she was always praying to God and saying, "God, please let me learn to read so that I can read the Bible." She recalled a missionary woman whom the Presbyterian Church sent to the small town of Mayesville, South Carolina, where she lived. This woman taught the black children to read and write.

She remembered getting up very early in the mornings and walking the five miles to school each day, carrying a small tin pail filled with leftovers from the supper meal. When she returned in the evenings, she would gather her family members around the table, and under a dim lamp, she taught them everything she had learned that day.

She remembered receiving scholarships, one to Scotia Institute in Concord, North Carolina, and one to Moody Bible Institute in Chicago.

Looking out of the smoky window of the train, as she passed through the small towns, she saw the ragged black children playing along the dirt roads, and she renewed her vow to educate them. This would help alleviate their poverty.

When she arrived in Daytona, she had $1.50 in her purse. Stepping from the train and looking around, she lifted her eyes to the heavens and said, "Dear God, with your help, I will build a school."

It was not easy for Mrs. Bethune. She went to the black families in the community and told them of her plans to educate their children, especially the girls. She felt the boys and men could always find work. She found an old battered bicycle put a basket on it. Then she begged for the ingredients to make sweet potato pies. After many days of riding all over Daytona peddling her pies, she finally had enough money to rent a small house on Palm Street. Here she started her school.

On October 3, 1904, with five little girls, Mrs. Bethune opened her school. She named it the Daytona Normal and Industrial School for Girls. She taught these girls to read and to write. She used sharpened charred sticks for pencils and the juice of the elderberry for ink. She taught them spiritual songs to sing. Soon they were invited to sing in the lobbies of grand hotels for the rich millionaires visiting Daytona. They received contributions when they sang.

Within two years her school had increased from five girls to 250 students. She desperately needed a larger building. Lifting her eyes to the heavens, as she always did when she needed strength, she prayed, saying, "Dear God, please show me where I can build my school." She stood so still and became so quiet, she could feel her prayers being answered.

Soon she found the site to build her school. It was a dump known as Hell's Hole on the edge of the black community. There was even a shack on the land that she could use. Mrs. Bethune found the owner of the property and asked if she could use the property for her school. He told her he would sell it to her for two hundred dollars. She did not have two hundred dollars, so she asked him to let her pay five dollars a month until she had paid it in full. He agreed.

Here on this dump, where the school stands to this day, she continued to teach girls to read, cook, and sew. She knew that this would best prepare them to earn a living, because it would be years before the business world would be ready for them.

One winter, while vacationing in Daytona, Thomas H. White of the White Sewing Machine Company was wandering in the area of the school. He saw children moving around this shack on the dump. He went inside and saw Mrs. Bethune sitting behind a desk made of crates.

He said to her, "What is this?"

She stood, so stately and proud, and then she said, "This is my school. I am Mrs. Mary McLeod Bethune, and I am teaching these children how to read and write and make a living for themselves."

He became so interested in what she told him that he emptied all of his pockets and then promised her he would be back. In his will, he left the school $67,000. Other millionaires, like John D. Rockefeller, Henry J. Kaiser, and James Proctor of the Proctor and Gamble Company, along with many others, made contributions to the school.

The first school building on this site was named Faith Hall. Before it was finished, Mrs. Bethune moved in. Her girls lived on the second floor and her office was on the first floor, a dirt floor. The boys, who were now also attending her school, lived with families in the community.

On the weekends, the fathers made improvements to supplement their children's tuition. Realizing that this building would need toilets, she went around asking the white plumbers to put them in. They laughed at her, saying, "What for? They'll never learn how to use them."

By now Mrs. Bethune was not easily intimidated. She only looked toward the heavens as toilets were put into the building.

But there were others watching with evil thoughts as Mrs. Bethune went about her work. She was now encouraging her children's families to register to vote. A message was sent to her to stop doing this or her building would be destroyed by fire. Did this stop her? No!

One night about eighty men on horseback and in Model-A cars rode out to her school. They had white hoods over their heads and white cloaks over their bodies. Their car horns were blasting and their horses were snorting and pawing the dirt. They were members of the Ku Klux Klan. They built a cross in front of her building and set it afire. The girls and Mrs. Bethune were on the second floor. They rushed to the window and looked out. They saw the men pouring buckets of kerosene around the wooden building. The girls began to scream and cry. Mrs. Bethune wrapped her arms around as many of the girls as she could as others stood behind her. In her strong contralto voice, she began to sing one of her favorite hymns: "Be not dismayed what-e'er betide, God will take care of you!" After a moment, the girls joined her. They sang one spiritual song after another. The men did not move. They sat there as if made of stone.

A dark cloud covered the sky. Lightning flashed through the palm and oak trees. The thunder began to roar with the sound of bass drums. Not one match was struck. No one knew when these men, with their hoods and cloaks, left the grounds, but when the rains stopped, none of them were there.

The girls crept to their beds. After many years, those who were there loved to tell the story of how Mrs. Bethune sang those Klansmen away.

Many young women who lived in Faith Hall will tell you of how they had been in this building during some of the worst storms. The lights go out, and the building becomes so dark, and they get so still. After a while, they feel a strangeness surround them, and they feel as though they can still hear that deep contralto voice singing to them, "Be not dismayed what-e'er betide, God will take care of you!" And, you know, perhaps they do.

Note: Mary McLeod Bethune insisted on being addressed as Mrs., a title rarely used when addressing black women in the South.

© 1995 Elaine F. Kitchings

The Storyteller, A Winner

It was one cold, rainy night, and three women, a schoolteacher, a librarian, and a storyteller, were driving from a conference through the backwoods of north Florida when their car ran out of gas. They could not remember when they had last seen a gas station. After sitting inside the car for a while, their eyes adjusted to the darkness of the night. In the distance, they were able to spot the light of a lonely farmhouse.

Pulling their coats closer to their bodies and their caps closer to their heads, they pushed against the forces of nature and groped their way to the small house. They shivered and shook as they knocked on the door. Finally, a little old woman answered their knock. They explained their troubles and asked for shelter till morning.

The old woman listened attentively, and then explained to them that the house was very small. Just she and her husband lived there, and they had only one spare room. Two could share the one bed but the other one would have to sleep in the barn with the cow and the sheep. "Fine with us," said the three women, trying to decide who would sleep where.

At last, they decided to draw straws to see who must sleep in the barn. The schoolteacher drew the shortest one and the storyteller drew the longest one. Slow-footed and bent over, trying to keep warm, the schoolteacher headed to the barn. About two hours later, there was a knock at the door. It was the schoolteacher, complaining.

"I can't sleep out there with that cow and that sheep. They are just too noisy."

The librarian knew she would have to make the exchange since her straw was not as long as the storyteller's. How she dreaded leaving the warm bed to go out to the cold barn. As slow as a swamp turtle, pulling her coat collar up around her neck to keep out the cold winds, she made her way to the barn. She tried to adjust herself to sleep when she began to sneeze. Of course, the barn was filled with hay for the animals, and she was allergic to it. After trying to stay inside the barn for two hours, she made a beeline to the farmhouse, vigorously knocking on the door.

"Please," said the librarian, "I can't sleep in the barn. I'm allergic to hay and I'm almost sneezing my head off."

Well, this meant that the storyteller would have to go out to the barn to sleep. The hour was late, and the wind was colder. As she left the farmhouse, she pulled her coat tightly around her and stuffed her hands deep down in her pockets and ran to the barn. She saw the cow, the sheep, and the hay. All was quiet. After three hours there was again a knock at the farmhouse door.

This time, the old woman rushed to the door and opened it. Standing there were the cow and the sheep. The storyteller was telling so many stories they could not sleep.

"The art of storytelling has awakened my communication and language skills and has given me the ability to transcend the human condition."

Bob Patterson
St. Augustine

Bob Patterson was born in Newark, New Jersey, and raised all over the U.S. He moved to St. Augustine in 1967 and still calls it home.

As a folk performer, Bob plays a twelve-string guitar and writes songs of such quality and in such quantity that he has been able to earn a living doing just that. His first major recording contract was with Vanguard Records. To date, Bob has five albums and two CDs to his credit. He has appeared all over the U.S. in nightclubs, at colleges and universities, at folk festivals, in resort hotels and premier listening rooms, on radio, and on nationally syndicated TV programs. He is a cofounder and director of the Gamble Rogers Folk Festival.

Bob is married to his dear companion, Joline, who plays bass, sings harmonies, and gives him the space to create his stories and music. Bob has two children.

Old Ten-Dollar Bill

When I first met William Ellis, he was already ninety years old but had the ability to recall events that had happened throughout his life with a clarity of mind that was much better than my own, and I was only a little more than half his age. He was born and raised on the banks of Florida's pristine and wild Ocklawaha River at a time when our life and well-being did not depend on the automobile. To Bill, the Ocklawaha River was one of Florida's magical, mystical, and holy places. Bill told me that the Ocklawaha was created when a blue velvet ribbon fell from God's hair.

Bill's best friend and fishing partner was old "Doc" Zeagler—a man revered in Putnam County as the best can-do, will-do, old-time physician around. Bill liked to take Doc fishin' on the Ocklawaha, where he could always take him under some low-hanging limbs, then bump them with the oar so at least a couple of water moccasins would fall into the boat. He got a big kick out of seeing Doc tiptoeing around the gunnels of the boat until he could swat them out.

Bill would enjoy a real belly laugh, catch his breath, and say, "They're just those little copperheaded water moccasins. They ain't gonna hurt ya! Why, if they bite ya, they're jist gonna make ya a little sick."

One morning, Bill was fishing all by himself in his favorite fishing hole when he saw the biggest water moccasin he'd ever seen.

"It was just short of eight feet long and as big around as the fattest part of yore leg. It was colored like a blueberry," Bill said. "Yep, it was a real purty blue color, but my first reaction when I saw such a monstrous snake was to grab my pistol. I aimed it at the snake, cocked the hammer, and was about to squeeze off a round when I thought, That snake ain't botherin' no one. It's just layin' there. So I uncocked the gun and put it back in its holster. The more I looked at that snake, the more curious I got. So I reached over and picked up one of my cane poles and poked that snake once or twice. Well, nothin' happened. So I began to make long strokes down the back of that snake. Then an amazing thing happened—that snake rolled over, showing off his purty blue belly.

"With great amazement, I continued to stroke that snake. When I got home that night, I just couldn't get the thought of the strange events of that day out of my mind, and so the next day and for many days thereafter, I returned to my favorite fishing hole and found that water moccasin lying right there on that same bank. Each day, I'd take my cane pole and stroke the back of that snake until it rolled over and then I'd stroke it some more. Each day I got a little closer until one day I actually reached down and stroked the back of that snake until it rolled over. Then I rubbed down its belly too."

Bill paused and then he chuckled. "He 'specially liked to be rubbed up under his head. It wus almost as big as mine," he remarked. "Ya know, before long, I could actually hand-feed that snake with bream and shellcrackers."

Now, I know that Bill's story has probably conjured up a disbeliever or two. I had second thoughts about it myself until I heard how William Ellis got his nickname of Old Ten-Dollar Bill. And that made a confirmed believer out of me. So let me set the record straight once and for all.

About the turn of the century, word got out that you could catch twenty-five-pound large-mouth bass in the Ocklawaha River. So many of those Yankee boys came down to get in on the bass-bustin' action, and who do you suppose they hired on as their guide? You're right, William Ellis. Who better than Bill knew that magical, mystical river?

When Bill floated those Yankee boys past his favorite fishing hole and that snake was lying up there on the bank, he would say, "Look at that giant water moccasin! Ain't that thang nigh as purty as a peacock backin' into a Florida sunset?"

One of those Yankee fishermen voiced the consensus of all of them when he said, "Ma always said, 'Beauty is in the eye of the beholder,' and it must be true, for that reptile is nothing but hideous to me."

"You are ignoring what a purty blue coat that water moccasin is a-wearin'! Why, I bet you boys ten dollars that I will go up there and pet that purty snake with my bare hands."

Up to that time the biggest bill that any Cracker boy ever saw was a two-dollar bill, but there seemed to be no shortage of Yankee boys who were both willing and able to give up a ten-dollar bill to see a dumb

Cracker get bitten by a big water moccasin. In fact, there were so many of them that the local boys at Neon Leon's Bait and Tackle Shop started to refer to William Ellis as "Old Ten-Dollar Bill." Now, if any of you are not convinced that what I'm telling you is the tooth, the whole tooth, and nothing but the tooth, I urge you to consider how many ten-dollar bills you see circulating around here even to this day. Every one of them verifies the fact that William Ellis could, and indeed did, walk up to that giant water moccasin, rub its back until it turned over, and hand-feed that snake with bream and shellcrackers You still have your doubts? Then I suggest that you leave all of your ten-dollar bills with me, and I'll thank you!

© 1996 Bob Patterson

lugin@aug.com

"I believe stories have the power to teach, heal, and change lives, as well as delight and entertain. Storytelling has enriched my life, and I love sharing stories with people of all ages."

Diane Rooks
St. Augustine

Born in Atlanta, Diane now lives in St. Augustine, Florida, with her husband. She has three children and four grandchildren. She graduated from Georgia State University with a degree in psychology and a minor in information systems and earned her master's degree in storytelling at East Tennessee State University. She is a former computer instructor and systems analyst.

Diane is an active member of the Florida Storytelling Association, Southern Order of Storytellers, and Tale Tellers of St. Augustine and serves on the board of the Healing Arts group of the National Storytelling Network. She regularly appears as a featured teller at major festivals in the South and is the author of *Spinning Gold Out of Straw: How Stories Heal*. One of her personal stories, "Infinite Resource and Sagacity," appeared in the spring 1998 issue of *Storytelling World*, an international publication. Her telling style ranges from quiet recollection to energetic character portrayal.

Snitch and Snatch

Adapted from an old English folktale

Growing up in Palatka, Florida, was not easy—especially for a young boy whose parents barely had two nickels to rub together. He didn't start out to be a thief, but he had to take advantage of every opportunity to help put food on the table. At first a few small objects just seemed to leap out at him, and gradually he realized that he had become an excellent pickpocket.

He was always around on Sunday afternoons when people were having picnics along the St. Johns River and never missed a sporting event, parade, fair, or festival. He got so proficient that he could pick a pocket or a pocketbook or lift a piece of jewelry faster than one can blink an eye.

Eventually, he decided that if he was going to keep improving his skills as a pickpocket, he had to leave Palatka. He needed a bigger town with more people. Let's face it, there were not that many pockets to pick in Palatka.

So he moved to St. Augustine. The opportunities seemed endless there. He could go to the Old Fort or just down on St. George Street, where crowds were preoccupied buying T-shirts and pralines. All the tourist attractions and art shows made his work easy, and in no time his life was comfortable.

Enjoying his new status, one summer evening he attended one of the free concerts on the Plaza. While listening to the music, he suddenly had a sinking feeling that his pocket had been picked. How could this be? How could anyone pick his pocket? He looked across the crowd and saw a young woman leaving the concert. As the saying goes, "It takes one to know one." He immediately recognized the thief and started following her.

She had long, red hair with a hat pulled down over her ears. He followed her until they were alone on narrow Treasury Street.

"I'd like to shake the hand of the person who could pick my pocket, for I am the best," he shouted to her.

She turned to face him and knew she had been caught. She smiled her most bewitching smile, quickly returned his wallet, and started to leave.

"Hey, wait a minute. My name is Snatch. What's yours?"

"Snitch," she said.

"Well, Snitch, you should have a reward for returning my wallet," said Snatch. "I'll buy your dinner."

Again she smiled and accepted his offer. Thus began a friendship between the two, and it was not long before they were working together. Sometimes she would distract the crowd and he would do the lifting, and sometimes it would be the other way around. This new relationship made the work even more fun and profitable. After several months, they decided to get married and were confident that their offspring would be the best pickpockets in the world. After Snitch became pregnant, she had to quit work, and Snatch had to work long, hard hours to provide for the two of them. Finally she gave birth to a beautiful, healthy baby boy.

Well, he was healthy in every way except that his right hand was clenched and held tightly against his chest. No amount of coaxing or pulling could get the hand away from his chest, and it got no better as time passed. This would never do—he couldn't be a pickpocket if his hand was deformed. Snitch and Snatch hocked everything they had and took the boy to specialists—wherever someone sounded promising. They went to St. Vincent's Hospital and Mayo Clinic in Jacksonville and Shands in Gainesville. All kinds of tests were run, but no one could find a cause for the problem, and neither could anyone cause the clenched hand to move from his chest. Snitch and Snatch were broke and discouraged.

While visiting Snatch's mother one day, they were bemoaning their hard luck with the child. She said, "Why don't you take him to Doc Newton. Sometimes our old country doctors can cure things that all the highfalutin' doctors and their tests can't."

Although the young couple found this hard to believe, they decided Doc Newton's fee was nothing compared to those specialists' fees. They were now willing to try almost anything.

Doc Newton listened carefully but didn't have a clue as to what would cause such a problem. When he took out his old pocket watch to check the time, he noticed a gleam in the baby's eyes that had not been there before. He held the watch in front of the baby's face and began to swing it slowly on its gold chain—back and forth and back and forth. The doctor noted that the baby's eyes tracked its every move—back and forth and back and forth—and the little hand began to quiver and slowly move outward. The doctor stopped swinging the watch and turned to call the parents. When he did, the baby reached out to grab the gold watch, and out from his tightly clenched fist fell the midwife's gold wedding ring.

Central Florida: East Coast

This section of Florida starts with the world-renowned Ormond and Daytona Beaches and stretches to the south, past the Space Coast to Melbourne. Although this section of Florida is not untrodden in Florida history, today the majority of its inhabitants are latecomers.

Sandy Beaulieu shares two of her lighthearted "why and how" stories. Both Herrick Jeffers and Suzie Shaeffer give their readers goose bumps with their versions of two old mysterious happenings. Ada Forney's rendition of one of India's folktales will give the reader a chuckle and a clue to the storytelling that was done in her family. And, finally, Margaret Lawrence's original story is sure to bring laughter but few takers for her Cousin Cassie's cookin'. All of these tellers' contributions are delightful! You'll read them again and again.

—Annette J. Bruce

"Storytelling uses words to paint pictures that are limited only by one's imagination for the purpose of entertaining, teaching, or taking the listener and teller on flights of fantasy. It is an art form that has opened up a new expression of my creativity, allowing me to reach others in ways I never before thought possible."

Sandy Beaulieu
Holly Hill

Sandy Beaulieu was born in Massachusetts and has been a resident of Florida for twenty-five years. She received a B.S. degree from the University of Connecticut and in 1999 her M.S. degree from the University of Central Florida's Mental Health Counseling Program. The recipient of the Florida Storyteller Guild's Scholarship to Florida Storytelling Camp in 1997, Sandy composes music and accompanies herself on her guitar when telling stories and singing songs.

Why Florida Key Deer Are So Small

Ever see those itty-bitty deer they grow in the Keys? Ever wonder how they got so small? Well, here's the true story!

Once upon a time—as any good story begins—there were many, many deer living in the Keys. Normal-size deer, I mean. Then a terrible drought began and all manner of living things were dying—plants, trees, fish, animals, birds, reptiles. All life was perishing from the relentless heat and lack of water. The wetlands could no longer support life, and things looked pretty grim. So all the creatures, great and small, that were still strong enough gathered to decide what to do. They prayed to the great sky god for rain, day after day after day and night after night after night. On and on they chanted and danced as long as there was any strength left in them and until their dry, parched throats gave out. Week after week after week and still there was no rain, not even a cloud in the sky. But still the creatures danced their special rain dance.

Then one day when almost all hope was gone, there appeared in the sky a small, puffy white cloud that began to grow and grow and grow. Bigger and bigger and bigger it got and darker and darker and darker, until it finally was a great big thunderhead cloud. The blue sky darkened as the huge cloud now covered the blazing sun, blocking out its scorching rays. The still quiet of the air was broken suddenly by the booming roar of thunder. Lightning flashed brilliantly across the now-black sky. The air was filled with the sweet, fresh smell of rain—gently falling at first. Then harder and harder and harder, until it came down in torrents as it can do in Florida. At first the creatures and all living things rejoiced and danced and played in the rain. The plants straightened and the flowers bloomed. The once dry and parched land sprang to life. And all seemed well.

But the rain kept coming and coming and coming—one inch, then two, five, nine inches, and still it came. The creatures sought shelter, wondering if perhaps they had chanted and danced too long. Mothers gathered their young ones to shelter them, and all waited in safety to see if the rain would subside. All, that is, except the young deer. Not heeding their mothers' warnings, they went out to play in the rain. You know how youngsters can be sometimes. They paid no attention to what was happening but splashed in the rain day after day. Well, maybe you can guess what happened. That's right! They played so long in the rain that they began to shrink and shrink and shrink. At first it was hardly noticeable, but as time went on they got smaller and smaller and smaller. Then, thank goodness, the rain stopped, the sun finally came out, and the deer finally stopped shrinking. And that's the true story of why when you travel through the Florida Keys on sunny days, you will see those very small deer playing. For they learned their lesson and no longer play in the rain, lest they shrink even more.

© 1995 Sandra E. Beaulieu

How the Birds Got Long Necks

"Little Bob"—that's what we called him. Mostly, I guess, because of the way he bobbed his head up and down on his long neck as he walked across our backyard, and the way he bobbed his head in and out of the canal water catching his lunch.

Being new to Florida (transplanted from the North), we had never seen a flamingo before, at least not in the wild and up close. It seemed like such a strange bird to us, with its long, crooked neck and bright pink feathers! We'd known bluebirds and blue jays, red cardinals, yellow finches, and red-breasted robins. But most of our familiar birds had been brown or black and fairly drab. We certainly had never seen a pink one before, or one with such a long neck, long legs, and big feet. And Little Bob wasn't the only bird we saw here with a long neck. There were egrets, herons, and even cormorants. We began to wonder why there were so many long-necked birds here in Florida.

Then we learned the truth—they weren't always long necked. No! Not at all. Back when this great land was little more than a swamp and no humans lived here, all the birds had short necks.

The animals ruled the land, and one day they called a gathering of all the elders to elect a representative to go north and discover what lay beyond the swamplands. Since the fish could not travel on land to survey it and it was too far for the animals to walk, the birds seemed to be the obvious choice. But how to choose the best bird for the job was a real puzzle. Wise, old Owl came up with a plan that was judged fair by all. They would have a contest in which all the birds could participate. The animal leaders agreed—Bear, Alligator, and Raccoon cast their votes to adopt Owl's plan. Only Skunk disagreed, but in the end the others won him over.

Word was sent out to all the corners of this vast land we now call Florida, so that birds of every kind could have a chance to participate. Egret came, and Heron, Pileated Woodpecker, Cormorant, Bald Eagle, Brown Pelican, Osprey, Flamingo, Hummingbird, Seagull, and Tern. All manner of fine-feathered friends began arriving on the day of the great contest. Excitement filled the air as all the animals, reptiles, and fish gathered to watch the birds compete.

Because a representative should be beautiful, the first event of the day was a beauty contest to decide which one was the most beautiful bird of all. In preparation for the judging, Flamingo ate all the pink shrimp she could find, and her feathers turned a lovely shade of pink. Surely bright pink would be judged the best of all, she thought. Wood Ibis dipped the ends of her white wings into the dark, night sky, turning the tips black as the night itself. Contrasted against pure white, they were quite stunning. Egret stood in the sun, bleaching her feathers as white as snow. (That's how she became known as Snowy Egret in a land where there is no snow.) Blue Heron rubbed his feathers against the azure sky, just a little, to add to the color of his silver-gray plumage. And

Pelican soaked his feathers in the tannic acid waters that washed the cypress knees, turning himself brown because he thought it was the most beautiful color in all the world. Peacock spread his beautiful tail and strutted back and forth in front of the judges. The bird competition was a magnificent sight and quite difficult to judge, but the beautiful pink of Flamingo won out.

The second event was to see who could fly the longest. And so all the contestants flew around in a huge circle in the sky. Round and round they flew—hour after hour. Well, as everyone who has lived here any length of time knows, the afternoons host frequent thunderstorms, heavy rains, and high winds. The birds were still flying when the afternoon storm moved in. The sky began to get dark, the thunder roared, and the lightning flashed. And the wind began to blow, stronger and stronger. All the creatures soon realized that this was no ordinary Florida afternoon thundershower. Soon Big Wind Hurricane was over the land, with such force that it blew some of the birds right out of the sky. Others held on to palm trees and shrubs with their feet and beaks as best they could. And after Big Wind Hurricane blew itself out, those birds who were hanging on—well, you guessed it—their necks were stretched out long and their legs were too.

"See," said Flamingo, "I am the best one to send. Not only am I beautifully pink, but with my long legs I can stretch way up high to see over any high places in the north, and with my long neck I can peer down from above the clouds to survey the land below."

And all agreed that Flamingo was the best one to send. With that, all the animals, reptiles, fish, and birds had a big celebration that lasted long into the night, and, in the morning, they sent Flamingo on his way to discover the lands to the north.

So don't be surprised if someday when you are in the north country, you just happen to see a lone, pink, long-necked, long-legged, strange-looking bird flying overhead. And don't be alarmed—just look your best, for it probably is Florida's representative, spying on you.

© 1995 Sandra E. Beaulieu
daytonasandbar@aol.com

"As a child, I sat transfixed, listening to the stories passed around in my family about some of my more 'colorful' relatives. The Southern Lights series is my personal tribute to those stories and storytellers of the Lewis family. Through the telling of each story, they live again in the hearts of a whole new audience."

Ada Forney
Melbourne

Ada Forney, a fourth generation Floridian, was born in Vero Beach and now lives in Melbourne. She is a professional storyteller, singer, author, composer, and professor of storytelling at Brevard Community College, from which she received her A.A. She also owns Storytree Productions.

Ada founded the Voices of Story Storytelling Guild, is past editor of the Florida Storytelling Association newsletter, *Storytimes,* and is current editor and board member with the Florida Folklore Society. She is also the assistant coordinator for the Florida Folk Heritage Awards Banquet and storytelling coordinator for Barberville Pioneer Days.

Ada celebrates the Southern Lights series of family and Florida stories for WLX TV, WFIT radio, the Florida Folk Festival, and Barberville Pioneer Days, as well as for schools, genealogical societies, and organizations like the Florida Historical Society. She is also a story partner at Canaveral National Seashore, where she and husband Jerry create original story and song programs on CD about Florida's endangered species.

Ples and the Mule Eggs

The family trickster—every family has one, but my family had an exceptional one. The day he pushed his way into the world was the moment the first trick was played. The doctor looked down at the seemingly placid, quiet, new baby and said, "Miz Lewis, he shore is a pleasant-looking child." That was how it all began. Pleasant he looked and Pleasant Andrew Lewis he became. Though Ples, as we called him, enjoyed his tricks and they gave much laughter to those on the sidelines, they often brought misery and humiliation to his victims.

I don't know if you are aware of it or not, but a full-blooded trickster knows when there's a gullible person around. It's that inborn sixth sense that makes him wise to the frailties of certain human minds. And anyone is fair game to a trickster. I saw Ples con his own flesh-and-blood granddaughter out of a fried apple pie at a family picnic by declaring it was poison. Seems he was the only one in all the wide world who was immune to that poison and could eat that pie without dying. The child sat entranced as her grandfather transformed poison into apple pie right before her eyes.

Children were a favorite target for Ples's tricks. They were so young and innocent. I've heard more stories of Ples and his "heart palpitations" than I care to remember. You see, he'd sit up on the back porch in the swing and watch—or, rather, supervise—while the children were planting the new crops in the garden out back of the house. ("Supervising" was Ples's other natural gift.) As the day wore on and the heat began to build, Ples would break out in a fine sweat. When he decided it was time for a cool drink, he would grab his chest, moan real loud, and roll his eyes. The kids would all come running to see what was wrong. Ples would blurt out, "I'm a'coming, Mamma! I'm coming to see you at last."

The children would crowd around, tears in their eyes, afraid their

Ada Forney 31

daddy was a'dying. He'd bid them all farewell and just as his eyes began to close, they would shout out in unison "Daddy, don't go! Please stay here! Daddy, we love you! What can we do to make you feel better?" Ples would rally just a tad and manage to mention the nickel in his watch pocket. It seems that if the children would take that nickel and run off to the general store and purchase a nice, cold bucket of beer, they just might revive their daddy. One of them would retrieve the treasured nickel and hold it, tightly grasped, in a small hand. Off the children would run, as fast as they could go to the store. Then, without spilling a drop, back they would come with that bucket of life-saving brew. Their daddy would quaff it down and let out a contented sigh. He was all right—till the next time he got a craving.

Just down the road from Ples's house lived the Hughes twins, Billy Joe and Bobby. They were constantly the butt of Ples's jokes. Like his own children, they just never seemed to learn their lesson. They were sitting on the porch one day, watching Ples's oldest boy, P. A. Jr., plowing the field with one of the best-trained mules in all of Florida. The boys sat mesmerized as that mule worked the field, plowing the fertile ground in perfect, straight rows. Unbeknownst to them, Ples was watching from just inside the door. He was ready to pit his trickster nature against those boys once more and was just waiting for his cue.

Billy Joe turned to Bobby and said, "You know, if we had us a pair of baby mules, we could get work 'round here helping people out. We could plow little flower gardens, tomato patches, and I bet we could make good money at it too."

Billy Joe agreed and the boys decided they would ask around and see if anyone knew where they could get a pair of baby mules. Ples's smile grew bigger as their conversation continued. He opened the door and strolled out onto the porch. He looked down and inquired if he had heard right: were the two boys looking for baby mules?

"Indeed, we are."

Well, he, Ples Lewis, had the solution to their problem. He knew where they could get baby mule eggs. But it was a well-kept secret, and they must swear not to tell anyone where they got the eggs. After all, these eggs were the rarest commodity and cost a lot of money. Finally, Ples cut to the chase—he agreed that if the boys served his every whim for two solid weeks, he would give each of them a baby mule egg of his very own. The boys agreed. For the next two weeks, Ples lived like a king, with those two boys waiting on him hand and foot. The two weeks passed incredibly slowly for the twins, but finally the last day came.

Billy Joe and Bobby ran to Ples's house and demanded their reward. Ples was in a pickle. Where on earth was he going to find a mule's egg? After all, mules don't come from eggs. Well, Ples took off for the big general store. Maybe he could find something that he could give to the boys to satisfy their demands. Well, it was truly his lucky day. There, in the window of the store, for the first time ever, were two of the largest coconuts Ples had ever seen. They had been traded in by a peddler from Key West. Ples knew those boys had never been to south Florida and figured they'd never seen a coconut. He looked at the coconuts with an analytical eye. They were brown, fuzzy like a mule's hide, egg-shaped, and hard as brickbats. Perfect, he thought. Ples bought those two coconuts, wrapped them carefully in moss, and took them home to the boys.

Billy Joe and Bobby could hardly believe their eyes. They cradled those "mule eggs" carefully in their arms and promised never to tell where they got this wonderful gift. They listened as Ples told them they would have to sit on the eggs and keep them warm every day for fourteen days. Dollar signs lit up in the boys' eyes as they imagined all the money they could make with their baby mules. They took the eggs home and after a short time sitting on those hard, prickly coconuts, an idea occurred to Bobby. He slipped out to the chicken coop and borrowed one of their daddy's egg incubators. They carefully placed the mule eggs inside the incubator and waited.

A secret told to a child is not kept for long, especially if there is money to be made. Soon, long lines of schoolchildren were paying a penny apiece to look at the boys' miraculous discovery—genuine "mule eggs." Billy Joe and Bobby's mamma became a tad suspicious at the sudden popularity of her boys. She sent their older brother, R. J., to find out what on earth those boys were up to this time. It wasn't long till he had a clean confession. He really tried to set the boys straight, but they would have none of it.

"These here things are mule eggs. You just wait one more week and you'll see!"

Well, two weeks later the "eggs" had still not hatched. The boys finally had to admit that R. J. might be right. They reached down into that incubator, picked up those mule eggs, and headed off to their favorite pitching hill. They stood a minute at the top of the small hill, took careful aim at the big old oak tree at the bottom, then hurled those eggs toward it. One of the eggs hit that tree and shot off at a sharp angle. It entered the briar patch next to the oak and scared a pair of young rabbits out of three months' growth. They ran around in circles in and out of that briar patch, then bounded off into the wild blue yonder. The boys looked down from the top of the rise and saw a creature with long, furry ears and powerful hind legs.

Billy Joe turned to his brother and said, "Mr. Lewis was right. Look it there, Billy Joe, there goes our baby mules!"

The Hughes twins swear to this very day that they were once the "possessors of the world's one and only pair of genuine baby mule eggs, supplied by that best-known purveyor of old trickster wisdom, Mister Pleasant A. Lewis."

Ples has passed on now, but he probably looks down on those boys from heaven and a gleam comes to his eye. I wonder if Ples has tried that one up there in heaven yet? If he did, I hope God has a sense of humor. If not, I'm sure that the Devil is being given a run for his money down below. As a matter of fact, I did hear that the old boy has a new supervisor and that he's right good at his job—except for the occasional heart palpitation.

© 1996 Ada Forney
storytree1@aol.com

"I believe stories and storytellers help bring understanding from past generations to the new ones."

Herrick Jeffers
Melbourne Village

A native of Rhode Island, Herrick has made Florida his home since 1963. He first lived in Tampa on the west coast and now makes his home in Melbourne on the east coast.

Herrick was an educator who used storytelling in every phase of a varied education career. He has been an instructor of chemistry and physics, a specific learning disabilities clinician, a school administrator, a rancher of lead-free armadillos, and a storyteller. He holds a master's degree in Storytelling from East Tennessee State University, where his thesis was a study of the beginnings and endings of traditional folk tales of various cultures.

Herrick has been involved in the Florida Storytellers Guild for many years. Barbara, his wife of more than forty-two years, is a listener and sounding board for the development of his stories.

Kissimmee Bound

Mysterious happenings are not unknown in Florida even today, but ninety years ago much of the state of Florida was uninhabited. And there were dangers in this vast wilderness—some common ones, others difficult to imagine. Fortunately, there were benevolent forces as well. This is my retelling of an old mystery tale.

Stanley and Victoria made an early start for Kissimmee. They knew that it was a farmer's day's ride by horse-drawn wagon from their farm in Rockledge to the home of Vicki's parents in Kissimmee, but with their good horse and better luck, Stan figured they could make it. With the stars still visible in the pre-dawn sky, they loaded their things into the wagon and started off with excitement and anticipation.

In 1905, Stan and Vicki signed on to homestead one of the sites along the edge of the Indian River close to the new community of Rockledge. For two years they had worked hard building their home and clearing the acreage that the contract required, but for them the years had been full of joy and peace as well. Both Vicki and Stan had many chores to do each day, which made it difficult to be away from the farm. However, in late October, to Vicki's delight, Stan made arrangements with the neighbors to tend the place for a few days. And so it was that the two young people, laughing and so much in love, set out on this trip. It was their first trip back to see Vicki's parents. Vicki's ripening figure told of the impending birth of their first child, and she wanted to be with her mother when the child was born.

The road to Kissimmee was only wagon ruts worn in the sandy soil across flat scrubland. The white tracks stretched west from the fishing village of Rockledge, crossed the St. Johns River at a small wooden bridge, and then wound across the open country for thirty miles to the cow town of Kissimmee. Clumps of trees, marking hammocks of higher ground, were scattered randomly. The hammocks were interspersed with palmettos and swamp. The dry fall period was a good time to try the trip across this swampy part of the country.

The sun was beginning to streak the eastern skies when the wagon creaked over the St. Johns River bridge. They stopped and unhitched the horse so he could drink from the river. Vicki gaily spread a cloth and unpacked a small basket of food for a quick snack. The freedom from the cares of the farm and the anticipation of seeing her family showed in her radiant face and in her joyful laughter. Stan quietly watched her and marveled at his fortune in being part of Vicki's love. Well aware of the fact that they had miles to go, they did not linger.

As the day wore on, the sky overhead became clear and blue, with a few clouds building ahead of them to the west. The sun beat down on the travelers during the heat of the day, but the horse pulled forward at a steady pace and the wheels squeaked in the sandy ruts and bumped over palmetto roots in the track.

Among the usual noises of the wagon and the monotonous drone of insects, Stan suddenly became aware of a new sound. It was a grating, rubbing sound coming from the left front wheel. He reined in the horse and climbed down. He grasped the wheel at opposite sides of the rim and shook it. As he had feared, the wood rim of the wheel had dried and shrunk. Now the whole wheel was loose, and sand was collecting in the joints. Continuing to ride on the wheel in this condition would soon cause the rim to come off and the wheel to collapse. Stan told Vicki about the problem, and they considered what they could do.

"If I had only realized this back at the river," said Stan. "We could have soaked the wheel then."

"Well, surely, dear," said Vicki, "there will be a creek or swampy area up along the road somewhere."

"True enough. But we may not make it to Kissimmee tonight."

"Relax, Stan, dear. We will be a bit longer than we expected, that is all. There is no harm in this delay. We can surely find shelter, if we need to, with one of the families at the old sugar plantation."

So Stan drove on, keeping an eye open for signs of water. Soon he spied a low, marshy area close to the road, and he turned the horse towards it. There was a small area of standing water just deep enough to cover the bottoms of the wheels. Stan drove the wagon into the water and let the dried wood absorb the moisture. Every few minutes, he had the horse move the wagon just enough to wet more of the wheels. All the time, Stan fretted about his inability to speed things up, but Vicki chatted happily and tried to keep him from thinking of the passing time. When the wood swelled and the wheels were tight, Stan drove back to the road and they continued on their way.

Now they would be riding into the sun until the yellow orb set in a blaze of dazzling golds and oranges. As beautiful as the sunset was, it served as a warning that night would soon be on them.

The responsibility for his wife and their unborn child weighed heavily on Stan's shoulders as the wagon moved toward the setting sun on this, the last day of October. He was not at all certain about this night—what might be waiting for them in the coming darkness. As the sun sank below the horizon and the short twilight period ended, darkness came like a velvet cloak. The few stars twinkled briefly and were eclipsed by the growing clouds in the west. Now the road was difficult to see, and Stan had to trust the horse to find his way. He sat with his arm around Vicki, holding her tightly. Night noises, only some of them truly recognizable, popped and snapped around them. An owl screeched from a tree. A distant snort indicated a large animal. The horse moved cautiously forward. A low rumble from the clouds signaled an unusual fall thunderstorm building ahead of them. There was a distant flicker of lightning that did not illuminate so much as agitate. A cry of a panther was heard, and the horse whinnied softly and stopped. Stan set the brake and climbed into the wagon bed. He and Vicki prepared a pallet in the wagon, and Stan urged Vicki to lie down. Some airborne thing fluttered by in the blackness. Stan covered Vicki with a quilt, and then, taking his gun and his lantern, he led the horse.

As they came over a slight rise, the wind suddenly gusted up and lightning flashed brighter than before. The thunder that followed was louder and closer. Then Stan saw the welcoming sight of a light. It glowed dimly from a small stand of pine trees not far off the road to the north.

"Look, Vicki, a light! Over to the right."

"It must be a cabin. Perhaps we can ask for shelter there," said Vicki, as she sat up in the back of the wagon.

Stan agreed, and, after helping Vicki back into the seat, he climbed up by her. Soon he found the white sand path leading towards the light, and the horse turned willingly. A few large drops of rain splattered on the wagon. In a short time the wagon stood by a porch that ran across the front of a small cabin. The soft glow of candles shining from inside the cabin silhouetted a table and two rocking chairs on the porch.

Sandspun

"Hello, in the house. Anyone at home?" called Stan.

An old man opened the door and stepped out onto the porch. "Mother, Mother, we have company," he called into the open door. Turning back to the wagon, he said, "Come in, come in."

The next flash of lightning revealed Vicki sitting on the seat of the wagon. "Oh, come, come, girl. Get down and out of this rain. Young man, take the horse and wagon around to the barn. There is plenty of room, for we have no animals anymore. Mother, Mother, poke up the fire. We need to dry these people."

Soon Vicki and Stan were seated by the fire. The old woman bustled about. Fixing tea and serving warm, sourdough bread, sweet-cream butter, and wild honey, she urged the young couple to eat.

The old man sat smiling happily. "Well, well, Mother. This is like old times when our children came home."

The storm raged outside, and the old couple invited Stan and Vicki to stay the night. Vicki said she and Stan would be glad to accept their hospitality, and Stan said they would pay for lodging, but the old couple would not hear of it. They spoke of how lonely they had been and what a treat it was to have visitors.

The next morning, before the break of dawn, Stan woke Vicki and helped her to the wagon, which he had brought around from the barn. Knowing that the old couple would resist any payment, Stan took two one-dollar bills from his pocket and looked around to see where he could leave them. He picked up a small piece of firewood and placed it on top of the bills on the porch table. Then they drove off to the Kissimmee road and turned west towards their destination.

The storm had passed, leaving the morning sparkling with clear, cool air. After about an hour, they came to a small cluster of homes. This was all that was left of what had been a prosperous sugar plantation, St. Cloud Plantation. A national economic depression and several years of bad freezes had caused the sugar market to crash and the operation to fail.

Stan stopped the wagon at the little market to buy some fruit for breakfast. The shopkeeper saw that they were travelers and asked where they had passed the night.

Stan said, "We were fortunate, indeed, to get shelter at the cabin of the old couple about an hour down the road. That wild storm and rain last evening nearly caught us out in the open."

"Storm? Cabin? We had no storm last night. And there are no farms or cabins down the Kissimmee road in that direction. The only house down there was burned to the ground almost two years ago. Killed old man Hatcher and his wife. But nobody has settled there since."

Stan and Vicki insisted that a couple gave them food and shelter, and the shopkeeper swore that it was impossible. Each was certain of the facts and not to be persuaded otherwise. Determined to find the truth, Stan and the shopkeeper rode back to look for the cabin. They came upon a grove of pine trees to the north of the road. In the grove there stood a chimney fireplace. Scattered in the grass were bits of charred wood—the ruins of a burned cabin. Beside the ruins, near where a door might have been, stood a metal table. And on that table, untouched by flames, were two one-dollar bills, weighted down by a small stick of firewood.

© 1996 Herrick Jeffers
herrickstr@aol.com

"Storytelling ties together all the activities I love—writing, reading, acting, and relating to other human beings."

Margaret Lawrence
Daytona Beach

Margaret Lawrence was born in Boulder, Colorado, and attended the University of Colorado. She didn't set foot outside that state until she married an engineer with an itchy foot and a desire to see the world. They spent twenty-three years living in India, Lebanon, Ceylon (Sri Lanka), Turkey, and Indonesia, where she discovered the magic of folktales. After many visits to Florida, she and her husband decided to make Daytona Beach their permanent home.

Margaret is a novelist (*Seven Thunders*), playwright (*Tiger Tales*), and storyteller. She is past president of the Florida Storyteller Guild, Inc. She has co-produced the Sandcastle Storytellers' Tellabration for nine successive years and has taught storytelling at the Elder Institute of the Daytona Beach Community College.

Margaret and her husband, Walt, have two sons, one daughter, and two grandchildren.

Cousin Cassie's Cookin'

My cousin Cassie got involved in the animal rights movement a couple of years ago. She has always been involved in one cause or another, so this was nothing new. But the events of the past few days have me concerned.

If I had to use one word to describe Cassie, that word would be *intense.* She is, without doubt, the most intense person I've ever known, and she is also a creature of habit. Every Sunday night, she invites me over to dinner. She loves to cook! And her first love is trying out new recipes. After dinner, she sets me down, digs her fingers into my arm, looks me right in the eye, and tells me about her latest cause with a capital C.

Her present Cause is—roadkill! That's right. Roadkill! It was an article in *The Daytona Beach News-Journal* that got Cassie started. The headline read, "Florida Residents Needed to Count Roadkill." It went on to say that if you would write to the Roadkill Society, they would send you everything needed to complete the survey. Well, Cassie wrote, and they sent her more information about roadkill than anyone ever needed to know. Now, don't get me wrong, I too hate to see those little critters lying in the road. Just the other day, I saw a little squirrel that had been run over, and it was squish-h-h-hed all over the road. (Hmm, I wonder if that's what they mean by ground squirrel.)

Now, the Roadkill Society wants people to gather information on the number of roadkills along the roads they travel. When you agree to become one of their roadkill counters, you have to fill out charts describing the route. They want to know if it was an unpaved road or a two-lane paved road and how many miles. You're also expected to observe the tallest vegetation on either side of the road, whether it is frequently mowed grass, or if there is concrete, asphalt, or gravel on either or both sides of the road—things like that.

And you are expected to detect hot spots! That means "multiple kills." For example, let's say you see several pureed possums near roadside garbage bins on trash nights. They want you to call up the powers-that-be and insist that those garbage bins be placed further off the road. That's so the little critters can go there and eat their little hearts out instead of getting them smashed out on the road as a part of a pavement pizza. See what I mean?

Well, you may laugh, but this organization does get results. Let me tell you about a survey they conducted in Canada. (Hey, we Floridians are not too proud to learn from Canadians.) In winter they have a lot of ice up there in Canada, and the road crews have to put salt on the roads to melt the ice. Well, you may not know this, livin' down here in Florida, but moose are attracted to salt. Those dumb animals would stand there licking up the salt, and a car or a truck would come along and—splat! No more moose! And sometimes no more car. So the members of the Canadian Roadkill Society persuaded the local highway department to use a different de-icing chemical on the roads, and now the moose stay in the forest where they belong!

There's a group in Texas that believes the animals should be taught to protect themselves. Once a week they go out into the prairie and chant poetry to the armadillos. Yes, truly, they do. I have it on good authority. A storyteller friend of mine told me so. It goes like this:

Oh, Armadillo, you're so sweet.

Please don't try to cross the street.

Now you have to admit, people who do all this to protect dumb animals are good people. And I was feeling good about Cassie getting involved with them—until yesterday.

Cassie came in absolutely steamed! She said one of the women she tried to recruit to help her with the survey just laughed at her, handed her a book, and asked, "Why don't you put all this killing to good use?"

Cassie shoved the book in front of my face. "Look at the title, *Florida Roadkill Cookbook, Featuring Flattened Fauna, Hushed Puppies and Thumper on a Bumper.*"

She was almost shouting. I don't think I've ever seen Cassie so indignant. She screamed, "Look at this book! Just look at it! The author thinks people will actually *eat* those poor little animals."

She sat down and started leafing through the book. "Why, it says we can all be roadside shoppers. In other words, we should go shopping along the sides of the road instead of going to the local meat market. It tells you how to shop, when to shop, and where to shop. And listen to this: 'A special treat is the Perambulating Pooch who didn't get out of the way in time. The grill of your vehicle serves to tenderize the meat.'"

At this point, I thought that Cassie might have a stroke, but then she took a deep breath, turned the page, and said, "It even has recipes," and she started reading them to me. "'Roast Rocky Raccoon: Brown pieces of meat and a sliver of garlic in butter.' Ooh, ooh, oh, my goodness! 'Poached Pelican: paprika, onions, bay leaf.' Mmmm! 'Curbside Cat: Roll pieces in flour. Sauté onion slices in butter.' Mmmmm."

Was Cassie licking her lips? No! Surely not! She turned the page and read another recipe—"'Gator Goulash Ingredients: gator stock, diced gator, chopped onions, season to taste.' Ooooh, yes." She was definitely licking her iips!

She went on. "Listen to this one! 'Owl Gumbo—Brown pieces of owl in large iron pot. Add chopped onions, one clove of garlic, one bay leaf. Add ground hog (commercial sausage may be substituted) and three quarts water. Simmer until tender and serve on rice.' Whooo!" she said. "Guess who-who-whoo's coming for dinner! I've got to go shopping!" Then she laughed—the strangest laugh I've ever heard. And with that, Cassie was out the door.

I've been wondering what she meant when she said she was going shopping. You don't suppose she's going to—no, not Cassie! On the other hand, she did say, "Guess who-who-whoo's coming *for* dinner!" She didn't say *to* dinner.

You remember I told you she invited me over to dinner every Sunday? I've just decided I'm not going over there this Sunday. In fact, I'm not ever going over there for dinner again.

"We use stories to explain our past, enrich our present, and express our desires, hopes, and fears for the future. Storytelling and story listening keeps us human."

Suzie Shaeffer
Ormond Beach

Suzie Shaeffer was born in Sikeston, Missouri, but her father's job with General Electric followed military contracts all over the U.S. and even to Japan and the Philippines. Suzie got sand in her shoes when she lived in Melbourne, Florida, as a child. She attended college in Florida in 1966 and has been a resident ever since. With a master's degree in library science, Suzie spent ten years as a coordinator of children's services. For eight years she published a regional parenting magazine and still operates a small desktop publishing business.

Suzie has been both a storyteller and puppeteer since 1973. She is known to thousands of Florida children as the StoryHat Lady and as half of the Kaleidoscope Storytellers in tandem with teller Terry Deer. While she performs mostly for children, she also tells tales for adults. Husband Jim and daughter Katie sometimes join her on stage as storytellers and puppeteers.

Suzie is a member of the Florida Storytelling Association and the National Storytelling Network and is very active in her local guild, Sandcastle Storytellers, serving as co-producer of their annual Tellabration since 1990.

The Silent Customer

This tale is considered an urban legend, despite its rural roots. An Alabama version was published by Maria Leach in The Thing at the Foot of the Bed and Other Scary Tales *(New York: Dell, 1959, 1978). Storyteller Sheila Dailey writes that she has come across several variants, including one from the upper peninsula in Michigan. Her version, "The Woman in Grey," appears in* The Ghost & I: Scary Stories for Participatory Telling, *edited by Jennifer Justice (Cambridge, MA: Yellow Moon Press, 1992). One of the oldest versions that I've come across is "The Tale the Crofter Told" in* Ghost Go Hunting *by Sorche Nic Leodhas (New York: Holt, Rinehart and Winston, 1965), in which a Scottish crofter and his wife find a ghostly woman milking their cow. When I crafted my version, it seemed natural to place it in the world of my sixth grade teacher.*

The sixth grade students were restless after lunch.

"Put away your arithmetic books," said their gray-haired teacher, "and I'll tell you a story."

"Is it a true one?"

"Yes, it is, and it happened right here in Melbourne, the third summer after I started teaching. Remember my telling you how I drove the school bus to earn extra money? Well, that wasn't my only part-time job. I also helped John Rawlins, the owner of our local grocery and feed store.

"Like the village school and church, the store served small nearby communities and did a thriving business. Mr. Rawlins was an energetic businessman, but he did not like paperwork, so he paid me to come in and do his bookkeeping. And when school was closed during the summer, I could be there all day to mind the store while he took time off to go fishing.

"Although Mr. Rawlins never told me what time I must be at work,

I was always there by sunup. When I got there, Mr. Rawlins would already have the doors unlocked and the stock arranged, ready for business. He usually left shortly after I arrived. I tried to get my bookwork finished before folks got their chores done and started coming in.

"One morning, as I was sitting at the counter with the accounts spread out in front of me, I heard the bell on the front door jingle. I finished the row of figures and looked up. There stood a customer waiting silently for my attention. She wasn't anyone I recognized. This was strange because between my teaching and working in the store, I knew every member of all the local families. And we did not have many visitors in the summer months.

"'Good morning ma'am,' I said. 'What can I do for you?'

"She didn't answer me but turned and walked over to the cooler in the corner. As I looked at her, I thought to myself that although she was young and had a pretty face, she looked ill. Reaching out with one thin hand, she pointed toward the chest. I opened the chest, and she pointed to a bottle of milk. I picked up the milk bottle—it was glass, not like the wax cartons you see today—and handed it to her. She clasped it to her chest, turned, and walked toward the door. I called after her, 'Wait, ma'am! You forgot to pay for the milk.'

"She stopped and turned toward me. That's when I noticed the dull expression in her pale blue eyes and how the pattern in her gingham dress was almost gone from too many washings and mendings.

"'Do you want me to put it on your account?' I asked.

"She nodded and was out the door and gone before I remembered that I didn't have her name, and so there was no way that I could put it into Mr. Rawlins' accounts receivable. I sighed and took the price of the milk from my pocket and put it in the till. Other people started coming in before I got the bookwork done, and in the rush I forgot about my silent customer.

"The next morning I finished dusting and went to the back to wash my hands. When I heard the bell, I called out, 'Be right with you!' I dried my hands and went out front. Standing by the cooler was the young woman from the day before. As I went up to her, I said in a gentle voice, 'I need to have your name if you're going to charge things.' She didn't reply, just stared down at the bottles of milk.

"She looked thinner than she had the day before, and her worn dress was covered with a gray film of dust. Quickly I reached down, grabbed a bottle and handed it to her. 'Here, you can pay me later,' I stammered.

Her eyes flickered up to mine. She seemed too tired to smile, but I saw the gratitude in her eyes—gratitude and a sadness so deep that I thought it would start me weeping right there.

"As busy as I was that day, I could not forget my silent customer. Her dark-circled eyes haunted me as I measured out flour; I thought of her threadbare dress as I cut a length of new calico. Sacking up a nickel's worth of hard candy, I started wondering if she had any children and, if so, did they ever get to have candy.

"I asked everyone I saw if they knew the young woman. No one knew her, nor had they seen any stranger around that fit the description I gave them. Needless to say, I took a bit of teasing for buying milk for a stranger.

"Yet my silent customer was a mystery, and a mystery was quite a novelty in our little community. When I arrived at the store the next morning, three customers were already there, and they didn't seem to be in any big hurry to do their shopping and leave. Mr. Rawlins didn't leave either. We were joined by half a dozen more shoppers in as many minutes. No one gave any reason for their early arrival, but there were a lot of quick glances in the direction of the front door. The low buzz of anticipation quieted at the sound of the bell.

"In came the young woman, gliding so quietly over the rough wood floor that her feet didn't seem to touch it. At first, those in the store tried to hide their curiosity, but when she ignored them, they turned and openly stared at her as she went to the cooler.

"When I handed her the milk, I asked, 'For your little ones?'

"The young woman was startled, and the look in her eyes reminded me of the eyes of a doe early one morning caught in the glare of my school bus lights. The doe had stood frozen for an instant before she whirled and bounded away from the road, followed by her spindly-legged fawn.

"Well, in a moment that young woman was outside the store, and it was those of us inside the store who were frozen in place. Then all at once, we rushed for the door, pushed and hindered one another till we got ourselves sorted out so we could run into the street. She was halfway out of town but still in our sights.

"At first, we tried to look as if we weren't following a stranger down a dusty street, but we became bolder as she paid us no attention. Soon we were past the schoolhouse and coming up fast on the whitewashed fence that surrounded both the church and cemetery. She turned as if to go into the church but took the path around the side to the grave-yard. We dropped back a ways then, hesitating to intrude on any person's grief. Still, we watched as she made her way back to a big live oak in the new section. The area was uncluttered by the tilting stones and small wilted gardens that crowded the front of the cemetery.

"She stopped under the big oak. Framed by its drooping branches and long beards of Spanish moss, she knelt and put the bottle of milk on the ground. Then, before our eyes, she vanished!

"Caught by surprise and disbelief, we gawked. We exclaimed! Then we rushed to the oak.

"We could find no sign of the woman or the bottle of milk—not there, or behind the tree, or among the gravestones nearby. We did find a marker by the tree, sticking up from one end of what looked like a recent grave. It was just a short wooden board with names and dates cut into it. As best we could make out, it was a simple marker for a young mother and her infant, buried there just three days before.

"The sun was shining brightly on that hot summer morning in Florida, but each of us felt the chill of a sudden cold breeze and witnessed a darkness as if something had for an instant covered the sun. Had we been chasing a ghost? Too shocked to talk about it, we avoided each other's eyes and started backing away. It was then that we heard it and stopped. The sound at first was thin and weak but steadily grew in volume until we knew it was the wail of a baby. And the sound was coming from the grave at our feet!

"We fell to our knees and started scrabbling at the loose dirt with our bare hands. Mr. Rawlins had more presence of mind. He ran to the church tool shed and got shovels.

"At last we reached the wooden box and, somehow, levered it up out of the ground. The blade of a shovel served as a crowbar to pry the lid off. Inside the simple pine box, resting quietly with her eyes closed, lay the body of my silent customer. In her arms was a squalling, live baby.

"The woman beside me reached down and gently took the infant from his dead mother's cold arms, cuddled and comforted the child. It was then that we saw, lying in the coffin beside the mother, two empty milk bottles and one filled with cold milk.

"In the days that followed, we learned that a migrant family was living about two miles north of Melbourne. They were poor and, like many in those hard years, could not afford the services of an undertaker. When the mother died of a fever, her newborn infant slipped into a coma. The baby seemed to be dead, and the grief-stricken family buried the two together.

"The Melbourne couple who cared for the little boy after he was rescued wanted to adopt him, but his natural family, as poor as they were, would not give him up.

"No, I'll never forget my silent customer. That young mother's love for her child was so strong that she rose from her grave three times to get milk to keep him alive until he could be rescued."

© Suzie Shaeffer
storyhat@aol.com

Central Florida: The Ridge and West Coast

This is probably the most cosmopolitan section of Florida—people from every state in the Union and the four corners of the world live in and visit this area of Florida

Two prize-winning cowboy poems are included for your pleasure. For the uninitiated, cowboy poetry is a newly popular genre, written about many subjects—from hat etiquette to balladlike tales and cowboy nostalgia. A number of books of cowboy poetry have been published in the past few years, and an annual Cowboy Poetry Gathering is held in Elko. Of course, Florida was cow country long before the West had a longhorn. Although "progress" has paved much of the pastures in this section, Marion County still has more than six hundred horse farms, ranging in size from ten acres to five thousand acres. With all these beautiful animals and farms, it is no surprise that veterinarian David Matlack has a penchant for cowboy poetry.

Cathy Gaskill likes Quaker stories, and the one included in this section is exciting. Sharon Johnson puts a new twist on an old folktale, and Mitchell O'Rear shares one of his dramatic pirate tales. Bill Wiseman, a great entertainer, lives up to his reputation with his two original stories, and Steve Brooks wrote, in his easygoing style, a "slice-of-life" story especially for this collection.

—Annette J. Bruce

"In 1997, I was one of several tellers who toured mainland China. It confirmed what I've long suspected—regardless of the culture, the skin color, or the language, storytelling will live forever and someday provide for true peace among the peoples of the world."

J. Stephen Brooks
Winter Park

When Steve was a small boy and his mama wanted him to explain something he'd done that he shouldn't have, she'd say to him, "Let me hear your story and it better be a good one!" So at a very early age, Steve learned the value of a good story, and he's been making them up and telling them ever since.

Steve has a B.A. in creative writing and an M.A. in teaching composition from the University of Central Florida, where he has taught. He has also taught at other public and private colleges in the Orlando area. He is the author of a collection of humorous, original tales, *Ain't Worth a Flip,* and also has a cassette of his humorous tales. Steve often serves as an emcee as well as a featured teller at storytelling festivals throughout Florida. He is a past president of the Storytellers of Central Florida, served several terms on the board of directors of the Florida Storytellers Association, and is an active member of the Southern Order of Storytellers and the National Storytelling Association.

Steve and his wife, Jean, have two children and one grandchild.

Three Little Words

"Thanks, Mom," I shouted as I ran out the front door to the park.

July 4, 1956, was a bright, sunny day filled with all sorts of adventure for a ten-year-old boy. We'd just moved to Florida from Alabama. Mom and Dad would bring the picnic lunch and join my teenage sister and me later in the day.

It was the first time since we had moved to this state of palm and orange trees that I'd been allowed to go anywhere by myself. I raced my shadow, marveling at the coconut palm trees that seemed to grow everywhere. As I ran, I made plans to get some of the coconuts that hung near their tops. Mom's coconut cake topped my list of favorite foods.

As I neared the park, I could hear kids screaming with glee. Then I saw them—all shapes and sizes, all ages. Some playing jumprope, some playing paddleball, or hopscotch, or Red Rover, Red Rover. There was a sudden burst of screams and giggles at one side of the park where the older kids were having sack races. A few kids roller-skated on the sidewalk. At last, at the far end of the park, I found a game of baseball, but I could see girls playing too, and I wasn't ready for that. What I wanted was to find a football game. Surely, they didn't let girls play *that* down here in Florida—if they did, I was ready to go back to Alabama.

As I stood there trying to decide whether to forget about the football game, suddenly kids and adults started rushing over to a bent-over palm tree, which must've been blown that way by one of the hurricanes I had heard so much about. I followed the crowd and saw that two small boys, maybe first graders, were holding the tree, crying. They must've gotten higher than they realized. And when they did, they were so frightened they froze. All they could do was cry. The siren from the fire truck made everybody jump. Gosh, I'd never seen a real rescue before, but they barely ran the ladder up before the two boys were back on the ground. The counselors made sure the boys were okay, and everyone went back to what they had been doing.

J. Stephen Brooks

I decided to make one more search for a football game, but football didn't seem to be in the plans for the day. Hoping to start a game, I approached a bunch of guys, but they were busy arguing about who had the guts to climb that palm tree.

"Man, you're crazy. Ain't nobody here gonna climb all the way to the coconuts."

"Well, it's been done. I seen Tommy Murphy when he done it."

"Yeah, but he was a teenager."

"So what?"

I seized my chance to meet them. "Bet those little kids won't try it again, ever. I'm Gus Roberts. Just moved here from Alabama. Y'all play football?"

"Sure, we play football."

"I'm a linebacker."

"I'm quarterback."

"Center."

"Halfback." The shouts were coming in as guys scrambled for positions.

"Hey, who do you think you are?" asked the guy who had seen the local legend climb the palm tree. "We were talking about climbing the tree, and you butted in."

"Hey, I didn't mean anything. I just like football."

"Yeah, well, wait your turn. As I was saying, I bet none of you guys can climb."

Sensing I was in the company of the neighborhood smart-aleck, I decided to call his hand. "If I climb the stupid tree, can we get up a game of football?"

From the dropped jaws, shuffling of feet, stammering, and throat-clearing, I knew I'd done the wrong thing, unless I intended to climb that tree. Of course, what they didn't know was that I was the champion rail-walker at my school back in Alabama.

"Yeah, go ahead. *I dare you.*"

From that day until I was man enough to ignore a dare, I became convinced that "I dare you" was this state's motto. But for now I had to show my courage and my cunning—I just wasn't sure where they were hiding. An older guy who had been standing back approached me.

"Hey, I'm Tommy Murphy. Just walk steady until the tree curves upward. It's bent over at such an angle that it's almost like climbing a hill, and there aren't any sandy spots. Take your time, then when you reach the curve, use the trunk of the tree to shimmy up to the coconuts. You *can* shimmy, can't you*?*"

"Yeah. Did you say you were Tommy Murphy? The local legend? Why are you giving me tips on how to match your record?"

"You'll just have to trust me."

None of the counselors were watching, so I was up and on my way to glory . . . or the morgue. It was easy at first, but the angle was deceptive, and when I was halfway, I glanced down and saw how high I was above the ground. That Florida sun burned me. Sweat trickled down my fingers, and my knees felt that they might collapse, but I knew this was my chance to either make it or become the laughing stock of that smart-aleck's group. Steadily, I made my way along the trunk, secretly thanking Mom for buying my new Keds last week instead of right before school started. After what seemed to me like hours but was really only minutes, I reached the part of the tree that shot straight up to the top— maybe ten or twelve feet to the coconuts and I'd meet the dare.

"Hey, kid, get down from that tree. Are you crazy?"

When the counselor yelled, I lost my cool and began to teeter. I fell forward, grabbed the trunk, and held tight. The crowd was as quiet as a graveyard, and every eye was on me. The only eyes I sought were those of the smart-aleck. They showed complete contempt, but as I looked at him more closely I detected a hint of fear—that I might actually do it. My confidence was restored, and I began to make my way toward those coconuts. In seconds I was knocking down coconuts. After three coconuts had been sent to the ground, I gathered my courage, dried my hands, and slipped back to the curve, where I steadied myself. After my legs quit shaking, I made my way far enough down the slope of the tree to a point where it was safe to jump. Rolling over and over, I was overcome with the sense that I really had done something worth talking about.

After all the pats on the back, someone showed up with a football. I put the coconuts at the bottom of the palm tree, and as I reconsidered whether or not that would be a safe place to leave my prizes, again the other local legend assured me with his words.

"Go along. They'll be here when your game is over."

As I cradled the ball in my arms, I knew that I'd hear again and again the challenge of those three little words. After all, Florida does offer many adventures, no matter what age you are. But don't take my word for this. Just go discover Florida for yourself. Go ahead. *I dare you.*

© J. Stephen Brooks

"Because I have witnessed firsthand the power of the spoken word, I am committed to improving the quality and quantity of stories and tellers."

Annette Jenks Bruce
Eustis

As the cofounder of the Florida Storytelling Camp and the Florida Storytellers Guild, Annette Bruce is often introduced as the "grand dame of storytelling in Florida." She is the recipient of local, state, and national recognition and honors for her contributions to the storytelling community. She has hosted fifty-seven episodes of *Annie's Gator Tales* (shown on local cable TV), recorded seven audiotapes, and is the author of *Tellable Cracker Tales* Volume 1, published by Pineapple Press. She has also recorded the book on a two-cassette audio album.

Annette, a native of Eustis, Florida, grew up in a large family in which daily stories were the norm. She and her late husband, John, have two daughters, four grandchildren, and two great-grandchildren.

The Jerusalem Apple

It was a lazy summer day—so lazy the fish wouldn't bite—so I decided to mosey down to Veasley's General Store, sit a spell, and hear a few stories, figuring, if luck was with me, I'd hear one worth repeating.

I was in luck. When I got there, a muck farmer from down southeast of Mount Dora had just started telling a tale that I found to my liking. As I walked up, he was saying, "It wus in late summer, and I b'lieve it wus in the year of eighteen twenty, when the folks in and all 'round Salem, New Jersey, got themselves in one more hullabaloo. It wus no news at all to them that their rich, young colonel, Robert G. Johnson, wus a mite peculiar, but his latest caper had convinced them that if the colonel's brains wus dynamite, he wouldn't have enough to blow his nose.

"It'd been twelve years since he made a trip to Europe and brought back Jerusalem Apple seed. He tried to get folks to grow the plants, even though everyone knew the apples wus as poisonous as a diamondback rattler. Each year, at the county fair, this strange bird offered a big cash prize fer the largest and best lookin' fruit grown on these plants. So the poor farmers grew the things, but they had sense enough to keep 'em a fur piece from their mouths.

"But now this weirdo wus sayin' he wus goin' to eat one of the poisonous things. Mind you, he volunteered to eat a deadly Jerusalem Apple. Furthermore, he said he was going to do so on the steps of the Salem Courthouse. He even set the time for the twenty-sixth of September at high noon. Well, sech foolish talk set tongues waggin' wherever people met.

"It wus plain to anyone with an iota of sense if Colonel Johnson did this he would be committin' suicide. But even if that wus his intent, sech an event wus not to be missed, so on the day set, folks came from near and far to see this nincompoop act the fool.

"Why, about two thousand folks jammed the public square that mornin'. Nearly every one of 'em said that Johnson wus jest wantin' to get a lot of attention. All of 'em knew that if he as much as tasted the deadly Jerusalem Apple he'd suffer a sure and painful death, and nearly everyone agreed he hadn't the slightest intention of doing it. But a few said, 'I don't b'lieve that he will drop dead as soon as he eats it, so he might jest taste it.'

"Dr. James VanMeeter wus the colonel's personal doctor, and he voiced his own ideas about sech foolishness. 'Why, if the colonel goes through with this, he will foam and froth at the mouth, and double over with appendicitis,' he said. 'All that oxalic acid! One dose and you're dead. Johnson suffers from high blood pressure too. That deadly juice will be sure ter aggravate that condition. If the Jerusalem Apple is fully ripe and warmed by the sun, he'll be exposing hisself to brain fever, and if, by some highly unlikely chance, he should survive, the skin of that Jerusalem Apple will stick to the lining of his stomach and eventually cause cancer.

"'I have given the colonel the benefit of my scientific knowledge, and my guess is that reason will win out. Johnson won't go through with it.'

"Someone yelled out, 'It's now high noon, and you see that he ain't here. He's makin' fools of us.'

"Minutes passed, and Colonel Johnson didn't show. Folks standin' out in the warm sun wus gettin' weary and hot. They began to hoot and jeer. Members of the Firemen's Band used their instruments to let everyone know that they didn't like the delay.

"At twelve fifteen the front door to the colonel's mansion opened, and he stepped out. The crowd cheered, and the Fireman's Band struck up a quick-steppin' tune. The colonel walked up Market Street totin' a basket on his arm.

"Colonel Johnson always stood out from the rank and file, but today he really looked different for he wus dressed in a tailor-made black suit, fashioned after George Washington's, if you please! Yeah, with white ruffled shirt, the three-cornered hat, gloves, stockings, and cane—the works!

"Climbin' the courthouse steps, he started right in with a long harangue about the Jerusalem Apple. He ranted and raved about it bein' a food fit fer the gods, and he told how it once wus popular in the diets of the Egyptians and Greeks then wus lost, and much later it turned up in Peru and Mexico. Cortez took it to Europe. And he hisself discovered it there and brought it to Salem.

"As the colonel spoke, he took one of the choice samples from the basket at his side. Holding it high, he watched it glisten an evil scarlet in the sun.

"'The time will come,' he promised, 'when this luscious apple will form the foundation of a great garden industry. For, truly, it is a delight to the eye, a joy to the palate, and altogether toothsome whether fried, baked, broiled, or eaten raw.'

"He rambled on and on. The folks were really gettin' weary and out of sorts.

"At last, he concluded his speech by saying, '. . . and to help dispel the scandalous stories, the wretched tales, and the despicable lies about this glorious and wonderful fruit, to prove to you once and for all that it is not poisonous and will not strike you dead, I am going to eat one right now.'

"The square got as silent and still as a graveyard. The colonel made a few fancy motions as he brought the Jerusalem Apple to his lips and— tuk a big bite.

"A woman screamed and fainted into the dust of the street. No one gave her a glance. All eyes were fastened on Colonel Johnson as he tuk one bite after another. He et the entire apple! He reached into the basket, got out another, and et it! Then he raised his hands high, turned 'round, and gave the crowd a big smile.

"Well, them folks went wild. They clapped, whistled, and shrieked. Dr. VanMeeter snapped shut his medical kit, jammed his hat over his ears, and took off down the street. The Firemen's Band blared wild music, and men and women danced in the streets.

"The crazy Colonel Johnson, first citizen of Salem, had defied the warnings of all of them educated men and proved that this fruit wus fit to eat.

"But then an argument broke out over the proper name of the fruit. It's most popular name wus the Jerusalem Apple, but some folks called it the Wolf Peach and still others, the Love Apple."

The old farmer stopped, filled and lit his pipe. I waited with baited breath for him to give us more information on this Jerusalem Apple, and I guess everyone else felt the same way for no one broke the spell. After blowing a few smoke rings, he started kind of reflecting and ruminating.

"Yes, this was in eighteen twenty. It was about this time that Spain ceded Florida to the United States, for it was in eighteen twenty that a ship carrying five million dollars in gold paid to Spain by the United States went down up here near the mouth of the Suwannee River. And as far as we know, that gold is still out there in the Gulf of Mexico. Yep, eighteen twenty—more than one hundred seventy-five years ago, and the states, united and otherwise, had already celebrated more than fifty birthdays.

"But Florida, the oldest territory by exploration, didn't become a state for another twenty-five years. And I understand that now Florida ranks second 'mong all the states in the production of this fruit or vegetable, which has become the foundation of a great garden industry. In fact, I've been told that it's Florida's number one vegetable crop. And, today, the only question concerning its name is: Do you pronounce it to-*may*-to or to-*mah*-to?"

Author's note: My thanks to Jean McGuire, Reference Librarian at the Eustis Memorial Library, for the statistics on Florida tomato production.

© 1995 Annette J. Bruce

Cracker Jake

Jacob Summerlin, the first white child born in Florida after Spain ceded the territory to the U.S., could ride a horse and crack a whip when he was eight years old. He grew up to be a top-notch cow-hunter and one of the wealthiest men in Florida. He was dubbed "King of the Crackers," but he referred to himself as Cracker Jake. He neither drank, smoked, nor gambled. He seemed to care little for money, but he could not and would not be shortchanged in a trade. He was a hard-working man of integrity and earned the respect of both his friends and enemies. He was generous and did many good deeds, of which only a few were ever recorded. These are well-documented facts concerning one of Florida's well-known pioneers and are the basis for this fictional ode to him.

We still have cowboys but no cow-hunters, cattle drives but no snail-pacing to keep them alive, and even the old hand-operated water pump is seldom seen today. Not many of us Crackers are still around who remember when it was considered bad luck to take a woman along on a cattle drive. (For years, I thought that bit of nonsense was started and kept alive by some egotistical male chauvinist, but then I found that it weren't the men's idea at all. Some women who were a whole lot smarter than I was kept that story alive so they could take it easy while their husbands were on the cattle drives. There wus more than one of us women who could ride a horse with the best of 'em, handle a gun, crack a whip, and cook up a satisfyin' pot of slum-gully.)

I better explain how the old water pump worked—it didn't! No, it didn't unless you poured water into the container at the top while someone worked that handle. This would form a suction to draw the underground water to the surface. Of course, if the gasket or washer wus no good or the pump pipe did not reach the underground water, it still didn't work and the water used for the prime was lost.

I needed to tell ya about the pump because all the talk lately about our needing rain reminded me of the time that Slim was shorthanded and hired me on to drive the chuck wagon for a cattle drive at a time when we really needed rain.

Cracker Jake

We were six days southeast of Homosassa,
Snail-pacing a thirsty herd to Punta Rassa,
When muck-fires and smoke magnified our woes
And parched us all, clean down to our toes!

Awesome was the Manatee River bed—
'Twas bone dry—all the fish and mammals dead!
As we dogged on under the blazing sky,
We found that even gator holes were dry.

All water was gone for our stock and men,
Then before our eyes 'peared a holding pen.

Annette Jenks Bruce

On the edge of a nearby cypress head,
Stood a water pump, painted a bright red.

When the men saw it, they started to cuss.
They figured that the devil was mocking us.
But Slim read a note tacked up nearby,
He read, "I know this pump looks mighty dry,

"But my friend, there is water down below.
I'm Cracker Jake, and believe me, I know!
There's a jug of water to prime the pump,
Buried on the north side of this here stump.

"Don't go drinkin' it, or you'll never survive.
For you've gotta prime the pump to stay alive!"
We dug up the jug, uncorked it right then!
Why, to risk that water would be a sin!

But Slim repeated what was in the note,
"'Prime the pump' is what the Cracker King wrote."
We poured that water in and pumped with gust—
Heard gurgling and out came a stream of rust.

"Stop the pump or we'll have a stampede, men.
Get the cattle into the holding pen.
Jinx, the troughs need repair. Joe, lend a hand.
Move! Get your jobs done as quick as you can!"

A large shallow fire pit we quickly dug
And filled it with water from the stone jug.
We gathered the firewood in croaker sacks!
With rosin we caulked the water-trough cracks.

The men watered and bedded down the cattle.
And each one cared for his horse and saddle.
With food and drink in hand, Slim bowed his head.
He gave thanks. We meant every word he said.

That pump now gave us water cool and clear.

It quenched our thirst and quieted our fear.
Instead of being fried extra crispy,
Cold-water baths renewed our energy.

Slim called out, "The King has more to say.
His closing words we must hear and obey.
'Refill the jug and bury it for others' sake.
Thank you kindly.' The note's signed, 'Cracker Jake.'"

Yes, we primed the pump, though full of doubt.
'Fore roundin' 'em up and movin' 'em out.
We filled the jug and buried it for others' sake.
We thanked our Maker and praised Cracker Jake!

Yes, we primed the pump, though full of doubt.
'Fore roundin' 'em up and movin' 'em out.
We filled the jug and buried it for others' sake,
And we're still thanking our Maker and praising King Jake!

© 1998 Annette J. Bruce
sanky5@aol.com

"I am a Quaker storyteller and mostly tell true stories of Quakers and their testimonies."

Cathy Gaskill
Orlando

Cathy Gaskill was born on the campus of Fisk University in Nashville, Tennessee, and now makes her home in central Florida. She has lived in Florida for forty years.

Cathy has been telling stories for more than twenty years, having researched and written many of them. One of her stories was developed into her first novel, *Ruth's Gift,* a tale of the internationally known Jones family in the mid-nineteenth century. It tells of romance in its most gentle form, of the impact of Quaker values on Charlie Jones, and of how he chose to change his life in pursuit of his beloved.

Besides being a storyteller, Cathy has also been a teacher (beginning in a university and ending in a pre-school) and a public health nurse. Cathy has two sons, who grew up hearing stories of Quakers in Florida, including Jonathan Dickinson, John Collins, and John and William Bartram.

Jonathan Dickinson's Florida Adventure

In 1692, a strong earthquake hit the Caribbean basin. The earth shook and rolled, and great waves washed over the land. Port Royal, Jamaica, was the hardest hit. That bustling capital was almost destroyed. But one of the buildings that was left standing was Dickinson's store. The Dickinsons were Quakers, and people said, "God must really be protecting these Quakers."

Since the store wasn't destroyed, people were able to buy things to help rebuild and get their homes back together again. After the earthquake, Francis Dickinson restocked his store and had more customers than ever.

His son, Jonathan, who helped run the store, married Mary Gale in 1693.

"Jonathan," said Mary. "Thee knows I was almost killed in the awful earthquake. I don't want to live here and raise our children in Port Royal. I am afraid another earthquake will come."

So Jonathan talked about this with his father. "Father, I have decided I don't want to be a storekeeper here in Port Royal. Thee knows William Penn founded the new Quaker colony of Pennsylvania in sixteen eighty-two. I hear from our friends that Philadelphia is a thriving community."

So Jonathan Dickinson persuaded his father to help him set up a Dickinson store in Philadelphia.

Jonathan and his new wife, Mary, planned to leave for Philadelphia early in the year, when the weather is favorable for sailing, but their son, Jonathan Jr., was born in March. They decided to wait until the baby was about six months old before they attempted the perilous trip to Philadelphia.

In August, they loaded the ship with the things needed to stock a general store: laces, cotton and woolen cloth, hatchets, knives, hammers, nails, pots and pans, dishes, buttons, needles, fishhooks, casks of wine, rum, sugar, molasses, saw planes (that's the kind for smoothing wood, not airplanes), metal chains, candlesticks, tins of spices, salt, wheat, tobacco, pipes, hogs, sheep, and many other things. They also took aboard barrels of water, food for the trip, and five thousand pounds in Spanish pieces of eight.

On August 23, 1696, Jonathan Dickinson, Mary, little baby Johnny, a cousin, Benjamin Allen, and Captain Joseph Kirle boarded the barkentine *Reformation*. Onboard were eight mariners—one of whom was Solomon Cresson, on his way home to his family in Philadelphia— eleven slaves whom Jonathan Dickinson was taking with him to help run the store and his home in Philadelphia, and a very elderly, well-known Quaker minister named William Barrow. Twenty-five people in all set sail for Philadelphia.

They sailed past Cuba, and they sailed past Miami and Fort Lauderdale—of course, in 1696 these cities were not there. Captain Kirle had an accident and broke his leg. On September 23, while the *Reformation* was still sailing northward off the coast of Florida, a terrible storm came up. The captain was unable to get around and look after the ship in such a storm. The other sailors were frightened. It was bad enough to have a disabled captain anytime, but it was disastrous during a storm. They were sure the ship would sink.

William Barrow's faith and calm manner were reassuring to all aboard. He prayed with the other Quakers and said, "Let it be as pleases God, I am content. The sting of death hath been removed from me many years agone."

As night came on, the fury of the storm increased. The wind blew and the rains came down in torrents. The ship was tossed about, and all hung on for life. Suddenly, the ship stopped. It didn't go back and forth anymore. It was over on its side, and water was coming in, but the ship wasn't sinking. The captain assured them that they had been blown aground.

As soon as it was light, they checked and, sure enough, there was land. They were on a sandbar. It was still raining, but the wind had calmed. Even though the ship was wrecked, everybody was safe. They knew that God had been watching over them. So they took what was left of the sails, got into the small boat, went to shore, and made a makeshift tent. They unloaded the people, and the able-bodied men went back and unloaded all of the goods that were on the ship. They put the boxes and bales, full of the materials for the store, under the tent. Mary Dickinson, with little Johnny in her arms, and the others sat under the tent, sheltered somewhat from the rain.

They were all frightened because they knew that they were in Florida, which belonged to Spain. And they were from Jamaica, which belonged to England. England was at war with Spain. They also knew that this coast where they had been wrecked was the home of the Jobe Indians, who were reportedly cannibals. All of them could recall stories of other ships wrecked on this coast and of all the people who were killed by the Indians.

So as they sat there under the makeshift tent, with the rain of the hurricane pouring down, they began to talk about what would happen if the Indians found them. They decided that the one sailor, Samuel Cresson, who could speak Spanish would be the spokesman for them all. He would tell the Indians that they were Spanish, not English, that they were from a different Spanish colony where some were blonde and had blue eyes, like Mary Dickinson and the baby.

But they had a problem. William Barrow was a very strict Quaker. He would never tell a lie. He believed that a Quaker must always tell the truth. They were really afraid that if William Barrow said anything, it would cause them all to be killed. So they asked him not to say a word.

About mid-morning, although it was still raining, there was enough light so they could see one Indian and then another come over the sand dune down the beach a ways. Oh! Their time had come, they thought. They started praying again, much in earnest as they felt that they would soon be dead. The two Indians came and looked around. They saw the wrecked ship and the people who were so frightened they didn't move. Jonathan Dickinson gave them some tobacco and pipes. Then the Indians went away. Everybody felt sure that they would be back.

William Barrow calmly suggested that they have a religious service. Even the slaves and sailor were willing to take part in a Quaker meeting. We'll have one final religious service before we die, they all thought. They sat around on the casks and boxes under the tent. And since Quakers worship together in silence, each one praying inwardly, they quietly sat there praying to God.

While they were praying, in came a number of Indian braves. They circled around behind all of the boxes and grabbed each person by the hair. They put knives to their necks, but the Jonathan Dickinson party continued to quietly pray. After many minutes, at a signal, the Indians let go and started making motions. They pointed to the boxes. So the people got up and the Indians started opening the boxes.

Oh! Think of all the things that were in the boxes! Everything that you would have in a store. Things that the Indians had seen the white man with were there in those boxes. The Indians were ecstatic. It took them the rest of the day to pack everything back in the boxes, get the boxes collected, and take the people and the boxes back to their village. By this time the rain had stopped. The Indian village, called *Ho-bay,* was near what we now call Jupiter.

The Indians started questioning all the people from the ship. They tried to get them to say that they were English. Then, with the Spanish governor's approval, they could kill their prisoners and keep all of the ship's cargo. But the only prisoner who would speak was the sailor who could speak Spanish.

"No! No!" he said. "We are Spaniards. We are on a trip to supply a Spanish colony."

The Indians tried to trick them. They sneaked up behind them and tried to hear them speaking English. They shouted "Nickaleer!" at them. That was the word they used to mean Englishman. This went on for two days. In spite of their extreme fatigue, the prisoners did not forget and speak. Finally, the Indians decided that since they weren't sure whether these were Spaniards who looked like Englishmen or really Englishmen, they would take them to St. Augustine. There, they could ask the Spanish governor of Florida whether these people were Spanish or English.

They marched the whole group along the beach for many miles toward St. Augustine. They came to an Indian village of a different tribe called the Ais, near what we now call Vero Beach. They stayed there almost a month as prisoners with just a few pieces of clothing. The weather was getting colder and colder, for it was almost November.

Then they started toward St. Augustine again. Still walking along the shore, they got to another Indian village. The wife of the chief of this village was a kind woman, and she saw that the shipwreck survivors had not had much to eat for a long time and the baby was having trouble nursing, so she found an Indian woman with milk to nurse the baby. She also wove palm fronds into a windbreaker for Mary Dickinson, so she and the baby could stay warmer.

They had many other adventures as they walked on up the coast, but

I cannot tell you all of them. At last, they got to St. Augustine. Since Spain was at war with England, they didn't know what the Spanish governor would do with them. Would he send them back to the Indians or throw them in prison himself? They wondered if they were just jumping out of the frying pan and into the fire.

The Indians marched them into St. Augustine and told the governor that they weren't sure whether these people were Spanish or English, so they had brought them to him.

The governor looked at these bedraggled, starved people, and said, "They're Spanish," even though he knew they were English.

He gave the Indians gifts, and they went back home. He found places in the homes of the citizens of St. Augustine for the shipwreck victims to stay. Most of them needed to be nurtured back to health. There was only one person in the entire shipwreck party who wasn't hungry or sick. Do you know who that was? Yes! The baby, little Jonathan Dickinson.

For more of the story of Jonathan Dickinson's Florida adventure, visit Jonathan Dickinson State Park near Jupiter, Florida.

"My stories strive to increase mutual understanding and to help others (both children and adults) overcome their fears. My storytelling actively involves participants as a means of maximizing learning potential."

Sharon Peregrine Johnson
Tampa

Sharon Peregrine Johnson holds a B.A. from Indiana University with a major in Fine Arts and an M.A. from the Graduate School of Library and Information Science at the University of South Florida. In 2001, she completed an M.A. in Educational Technology Leadership from the George Washington University Graduate School of Education and Human Resources. She is a professional website designer and developer for the Information Technology Center at Baylor University in Waco, Texas.

Sharon wears many hats—web designer, illustrator/artist, writer, historian, and folklorist/storyteller. She has published writings on folklore, history, the Internet, and Western Americana. She has more than twenty-five years of experience in presenting programs and workshops on these topics and has done projects for museums and other educational agencies in Florida, New Mexico, and Texas. Married to Byron A. Johnson, director of the Texas Ranger Hall of Fame in Waco, Sharon also has other interests, including producing videos, playing the harp, gardening, and playing with her cats.

Monkey, the Trickster

A very long time ago, animals, fish, humans, and all living creatures spoke the same language and respected each other, even sharks and mankind. Shark was a noble fish of the sea, not the aggressive scavenger he is today. This story explains why sharks and humans are enemies.

In a land near the sea, now called Florida, there lived a kind and contented people. The Chief wisely led his people and the nearby animal and water kingdoms. One day the Chief's only daughter, Little Star, fell ill and was unable to speak or move. The Chief tried to find someone to cure his daughter of this strange disease, but each one gave the same answer: "The little girl will die." The little girl and her brothers were the Chief's pride and joy. Their mother had died two years before, and the Chief was very distraught over the little girl's illness.

A villager told the Chief about the Ancient One, a frail female elder who lived on a secluded island in the Atlantic and could cure unusual diseases with her special remedies. The Chief's oldest son was sent to bring her to the mainland.

When he returned with the Ancient One, she saw the Chief and spent the night with the stricken child, who lay motionless and was as pale as moonlight. By morning, the Ancient One knew of one possible cure, if there was enough time. As she went to see the Chief, she looked at the sad faces around her and spoke to the father.

"Indeed, this is sad, but I cannot cure your daughter's illness because I do not have the remedy here."

The father's lips quivered, and tears slowly fell down his face. The others were silent and sad.

The Old Sage continued, "Your daughter will surely die—unless she eats the heart of a monkey."

The Chief's land was large and had alligators, panthers, snakes, and a wide range of exotic and unusual animals, but no monkeys. Far to the southeast there was an island full of monkeys. It was a long and perilous journey requiring the fastest and strongest swimmer, and the Chief proclaimed, "Whoever will bring a monkey and save my daughter's life will be made chief of the fish."

Shark volunteered and everyone agreed that he was the best choice because of his speed, strength, guile, and cunning. He was proud of his abilities and knew he would be a worthy leader.

Shark left that day and swam straight to Monkey Island. Shark watched and waited for an opportunity to trick a young, gullible monkey. He overheard a young female monkey talking about how she wanted to travel and see the world. When he saw her alone in a nearby mangrove tree, Shark said, "Monkey, Monkey, I know of a wonderful land full of exotic fruits, endless beaches, mangrove and palm trees, and lots of sunshine and warm weather. Would you like to see it?"

"Indeed, I would," said Monkey, who had always wanted to travel. "I would like very much to go there, but I cannot since I do not swim."

"Oh, hop on my back, and I will give you a ride," said Shark. "If I take you there you will be the honored guest of the Chief."

Monkey could not resist such an attractive offer. So she replied, "Well, this sounds wonderful. I will go, but you must promise to bring me back when I ask."

Shark agreed and Monkey jumped on his back, and they were soon at the shores of Florida. The people of the village warmly greeted them. Monkey stretched her legs, explored the land, and ate the wonderful delicacies.

Sleepy after her long trip and full meal, Monkey climbed up and fell asleep on the limb of a mangrove tree that grew near the shoreline. The ocean water rose at high tide and covered the land beneath the tree. Monkey awoke to the sounds of small waves hitting the tree and of voices. She looked down and saw Crab and Shrimp talking to her.

"Thank you, my dear," they said. "You are so noble and unselfish. It is a wonderful thing that you are doing—giving your heart to cure the Chief's daughter. You will always be remembered and honored for your generosity."

The princess is precious but I have no intention of giving up my heart, thought Monkey. "Oh, no," Monkey said to Crab and Shrimp. "This is awful! I am so sorry. I do wish someone had told me before now. My heart is at home, sitting in my palm tree. What shall I do? This is horrible. The Chief's daughter is so young and beautiful, and everyone is expecting me to save her and I did not bring my heart. Oh, dear! What can I do?" And she began to cry.

Quickly, Crab and Shrimp left and found Shark. They told him, "Monkey said that you did not tell her that the Chief's daughter needed her heart, and she left it at home in a palm tree."

Shark found Monkey, who was still crying. "Come quickly," he said. "I will take you back to your home and you can bring your heart back here."

Monkey again jumped on Shark's back and was swiftly taken back to her home. Monkey ran over the sand and climbed to the top of her coconut palm. There she sat, eating and laughing at Shark. She refused to come down, and nothing Shark said or did convinced her to do otherwise.

Sadly, Shark swam home and reported what had happened. When the Chief's daughter heard the story of Monkey's trick, she laughed so hard at such foolishness that she was immediately cured.

Crab and Shrimp were banished to the ocean floor and made prey for birds, large fish, and humans. As for Shark, he was humiliated and became an outcast. And to this very day, sharks and humans are still angry with each other and remain enemies.

*"I especially enjoy animal stories where-
in our animal friends teach us about
that most slippery of propositions—
being human."*

David C. Matlack
Ocala

David is a part-time veterinarian and full-time storyteller, which makes for a busy and interesting life. He was born and raised in Indiana, where he received his Doctor of Veterinary Medicine degree from Purdue University in 1984. He moved to Florida in 1986.

David is a sought-after teller, emcee, teacher, and administrator. He was one of the founders of the Ocali Storytelling Guild and served as president for two terms. In his second year as president, he was the driving force behind establishing the Ocala Storytelling Festival. He served as festival director in 1998 and 1999. He has performed from Cedar Key to Nantucket Island, emceeing, conducting workshops, and sharing folktales, tall tales, myths, and personal stories.

From 1986 until 1999, David, his wife, and their three children lived in the Ocala National Forest. They have since moved back to Indiana.

Seek the Higher Ground

I see yer chaps is still rough, yer hands'r smooth, peach fuzz on your
    face.
You must be the young'n they sent to take my place.

That's well 'n fine; look like yuh kin work hard.
I've done my time; I'm jest plain tar'd.

Now, you'll mostly learn as you go; that's what I done.
When ta fetch 'em up, when ta let 'em run.

These cattle, they're a hardy breed—a sturdy strain.
Been on these swamps since this was the Spanish main.

So jes watch 'em real close; then drive 'em slow and steady.
When bossman Nate allows, the market boat's ready.

Oh, I'd share everyday's learnin' of this life iff'n I could,
But when I was your age, mouth teachin' never did no good.

Yeah, you'll do fine; pick it up along the way,
Learn some new trick or feat pert near ev'ry day.

But before I pack it up and pack it on out,
Why there's jes one thing I wanna warn you about.

When the saw grass sets in to flower,
And the sky is a changin' hour by hour,
Seek the higher ground.

David C. Matlack 75

When snakes and all kind vermin start to head north,
Every creepy-crawlie-critter pulls up and pushes forth,
Seek the higher ground.

When Seminoles, wise with lore of reading the sky,
Pass in droves, they pass you by,
Seek the higher ground.

When bands of clouds come swirling west to east,
It may be too late, but gather up ev'ry beast,
And seek the higher ground.

When the pine trees sing and palm fronds fall,
And grass lays low that once was tall,
Seek the higher ground.

When the cane fields set in to moan,
Okechobee starts to groan,
When like a tide there's a'risin' on that lake,
And her dikes start to tremble and start to quake,
Seek the higher ground.

When overhead it's a swirlin' mess of blues and grays,
And it starts to rain and to rainin' sideways,
It may well be too late, yuh done jeop'rdized the herd,
But yuh made a pact with Nate, so keep to your word,
And seek the higher ground.

Cuz there's a storm a'comin' the likes of which yuh ain't never seen.
Make yer blood run cold, yer eyes turn green.
The kinda storm that's kilt a thousand sailin' Spaniards,
Sent to watery graves, clawin' at halyards.
Kinda storm that's sunk ships of fortune, ships of fools,
Ships of gold . . . ships of jewels.
Kinda storm that rearranges the arrangement of land and sea,
Mockin' 'r human efforts, makin' this good life . . . misery.

So, son, you see these signs, gather 'em up and keep 'em 'round,
Drive 'em to the north, drive 'em to higher ground.

Head for the ridge, head for the spine.
Drive 'em fast, don't waste no time,
Seek the higher ground.

And yuh stay there a month or more, maybe two,
Cuz these here swamps'll be a sea of blue,
So keep the higher ground.

There'll be death and stench and rot all around,
Putrid, sulfurous gases pushin' outta the ground.
Keep the higher ground.

Ev'ry known sickness, ev'ry deathly plague—
Malaria, yeller fever, bloat 'n black leg.
Keep the higher ground.

And the skeeters, aih doggy, the sky'll be black.
Head south too soon, they'll drive yuh right back,
So keep the higher ground.

And when it's all said 'n done, and ev'rything's high 'n dry,
You'll know when it's time, you'll know by and by,
When to leave the higher ground.

When the once-ill south wind starts to smell sweet,
It'll be dry underneath their feet.
Then leave the higher ground.

They'll fatten faster 'n ever; the grass'll be high.
The grass'll be good oncet hits dry,
So leave the higher ground.

Now, son, you remember this and you'll do good.
I'd learn yuh more iff'n I could.

But t'ain't nothin' like the doing; let experience be your map.
So I'll jes be going. I'll jes shut my trap.

David C. Matlack

And I shore ain't gonna tell yuh how to live your life,
How to pray, or iff'n and when to take a wife.

Ain't gonna meddle and pry where it ain't my place,
Ain't gonna lecture and preach to your coltish face.

Naw, yuh ain't got no use for my two cents,
So I'll jes wish yuh luck and God's providence!

Wel-l-l , come ta think of it, before I go,
There is just one more thing you oughter know.

When things go bad, and yer wantin' to take the Lord's name in vain,
Yuh wanna cuss and swear and sherk the blame,
When yuh git caught with yer finger in the pie,
And thinkin' there's no harm in tellin' a little lie,
When t' others come round with their cards and their whiskey,
And yer itchin' fer skirts and feelin' frisky,
When yuh jes git paid and got a pocket full o' money,
And lookin' to gamble or maybe take a honey,
When yer in Ft. Mars after a long hard drive,
And tempted by ev'ry saloon and red-light dive,
When yer strainin' to stray and Satan's sin seems all around,

Well . . . you know what to do—*seek* the higher ground.
Oh, son . . . *keep* the higher ground.

Author's note: The lore about an impending hurricane was inspired by passages from Zora Neale Hurston's Their Eyes Were Watching God.

© David Matlack
storyvet@infocom.com

"I think that storytelling is unique of all art forms in that it allows immediate interaction. No other performance art allows such close contact with an audience."

Mitchell O'Rear
Orlando

Mitchell was born in Chattanooga, Tennessee. His family moved to Tallahassee, Florida, when he was six years old and when he was nine, to Orlando, where he still makes his home.

Trained in the Carnegie-Mellon acting program, Mitchell O'Rear has performed for both young and old alike, mesmerizing audiences from all walks of life. Mitchell's performance experience includes programs at McKids Toy Stores and at the Mark Twain Memorial in Hartford, Connecticut. Each year since 1989, Mitchell has been selected for the Artist-in-the-Schools Program in Hillsborough County. He is a past president of the Florida Storytellers Guild and is serving as president of the Storytellers of Central Florida. He is the founder and director of "Ghosts in the Gardens," held annually at Harry P. Leu Gardens. He has perfected the jump story.

Gaspar

The long, narrow streets were quiet as thick fog rolled in from the sea, wrapping gray mist around shops and buildings. The dark evening was heavy with moist air. Shadows crouched around every corner, as the snores of drunken sailors echoed through the alleyways. Underneath the sound of the town clock striking midnight—*bong, bong, bong*—was the tapping sound of a cane and wooden leg from an old and bent man making his way quickly through the black and lonely night. The man was wearing a long, brown, hooded coat that concealed his face. He came to the door of a dimly lit pub and pulled hard to open it. The man was met with a wave of stale, smoky air and the loud laughter of a small room packed with sixty to seventy sailors from around the world. At the bar there was a heavy man with huge hands talking to a group of people gathered around him, mostly other sailors and a few barmaids. He was wearing an orange bandanna tied around his head and several gold chains around his neck. There was a gold hoop earring in his ear. The man was waving his sword over his head as he told a tale of a past adventure.

"And then, mates, I took my sword like this and ran it into the belly of the shark. Then the varmint pulled me down to the bottom of the ocean and began to gnaw on my leg. I knew this was my last chance so I dug my sword into his side and then I pulled it out and sliced it through his bloody face. Finally the creature was dead. I pulled him back up to the ship, and we had a mighty fine dinner that night. That shark was at least thirty-five feet long and weighed a thousand pounds if he weighed an ounce!"

"Yeah, and the last time you told that story, he was only twenty feet long and you said that you shot him with your pistol."

The crowd roared with laughter as the large sailor bowed his head and blushed with embarrassment.

"Well, Mister Fisherman," said Kelly, the pub keeper, "have a drink on the house. And next time you go to telling that story, make the shark forty-five feet long. Say that all you had to do to catch him was to hold out a little worm and wiggle it overboard for bait."

The crowd laughed again, but as the old man entered the pub, the sound dulled to a whisper. As he made his way to the back of the pub, the crowd soon forgot him. The noise swelled to a high pitch. The old man went to a dark corner of the room and spoke to a thin, nervous-looking man sitting at a table and drinking ale.

The old man leaned on the table. "Are you Forester Smith from the *Tribune?*"

"Yes, I am. And you are?"

"Never mind who I am. Did you make the arrangements as I requested?"

"Yes."

"Then you have the gold with you?"

"Uh, well. . . ." Smith looked around the room and then back at the old man. "Yes, the money is with me as you requested. How do I know you are . . ."

"Shut up and listen." The man pulled up beside Smith and sat down. Smith tried to pull away but the man grabbed his shirt and pulled him close. "Getting a little nervous, are you? Now don't you go and try to sneak away from me."

The man pulled out a dagger from his vest and stabbed the table top so close to Smith's hand that it cut the side of his wrist. Smith pulled his hand away and saw drops of blood dripping onto the table.

"Look what you've done." Smith pulled out a handkerchief and wrapped his wrist to stop the bleeding.

He looked around the room for help and saw nothing but coarse, crude men who had lived hard lives at sea. Most of them were cut and bruised with scars on their faces and arms. Some of the men were missing hands or fingers. All of them were drunk with rum. If the old man had stabbed Smith in the heart and killed him, none of the men in this room would have cared. Smith was frightened but he knew that there was nothing else for him to do but listen to the old man's story. He looked back at the old man. "Please, let go of my shirt and I will listen to what you have to say."

"And you are sure you have the gold? Let me see it!"

"Here, among this crowd?"

"I'm not afraid of anyone here. Let me see the money."

Smith pulled out a small sack of gold coins and showed it to the man. He quickly put it back into his pocket. "You do understand that the information you are about to give me has to be accurate before we can print it in the paper."

The old man pulled the knife out of the table and caressed his cheek with the cold, flat side of the blade. He smiled a big grin, exposing his yellowed teeth, the two in front capped in gold. He took a swig of rum from the bottle on the table, stared out into the darkness of the pub, and was silent for a moment.

"You see, it all began one gloriously fine day many years ago on the island of Captiva. We had gotten word that a Spanish galleon was headed our way. It was loaded with gold and jewels and wasn't supposed to be heavily armed. We all knew that it would be easy prey, and we were anxious for another conquest. There hadn't been a ship in these waters for at least six months. We had nothing left but the worst provisions. Our food supplies were low and we had no rum to drink. The crew was getting anxious, and fights were breaking out nightly. So at mid-afternoon, when the lookout spotted the ship five miles off our coast, the crew broke out singing and laughing. We were all ready for a good fight.

"It was the largest galleon I had ever seen. The ship was heavy and moved slowly through the water. I could tell it was rich with treasure. The first mate ran to tell our captain, José Gaspar, the most notorious pirate on the Spanish main, the news of the ship.

"'Captain, the ship has been spotted off the coast five miles away.'

"'Then time's a'wastin', lad. Prepare the ship to sail.'

"'Aye, aye, Captain!'

"There was a swarm of men on the shoreline running around like bees getting ready to attack. We loaded twenty-five cannons aboard the ship, and our entire artillery of guns, and sixty kegs of gunpowder.

"There was fire in the eyes of every man and lust in our hearts. Gaspar was the last to board the ship. He was a small but powerful man who always wore the finest of clothes. Underneath the red velvet coat was a heart of stone. Beneath his plumed hat was a mind capable of the most horrible acts of murder and mayhem. He never had a moment's regret for the violence and destruction he left in his wake. His crews were the most bloodthirsty sailors ever to sail on the Spanish main. They served him with complete loyalty, for even they were afraid of Gaspar—Gasprilla, as he called himself. On his face was the scar of a five-pointed star that he had carved underneath his left eye. Often, just before he took the life of some poor soul, he would take the tip of his knife and brand him with the same mark.

"Gaspar stepped aboard the ship. He swung six pistols over his shoulder. Two cutlasses, sharp and shiny, were hanging at his waist, and four daggers were tucked into his belt. He yelled to the men as he made his way to the bridge, 'Onward, ho, mates. There is no stopping us now.'

"It took twenty men to lift the sails. As the wind caressed our ship and pushed us forward, we all shouted battle cries. We were on our way. Our cannons were hidden from sight with canvas cloths. We flew the American flag to disguise our ship. We would only raise the black flag when we were close enough to attack. By the time a ship's crew saw the skull and crossbones hanging from our mast, it would be too late for them to escape. As we began our conquest, the sun was beginning to set. The sky had a soft, red glow—soon it would be burning with fire. It would be filled with black smoke from our cannons and guns. Horror-filled screams would echo in the wind.

"Our prey was sitting in the middle of the ocean, full of treasure, just waiting for us. Our ship hovered around the Spanish galleon like a shark ready to tear its teeth into the flesh of its victim. The sun finally set. The night sky was black as pitch. We were filled with excitement as we waited breathlessly. Silently we pulled up next to the ship. We threw up our rope ladders and ascended onto the deck. With swords raised and guns aimed, we were ready for blood. One hundred of our men were aboard the ship within moments. We scouted out the deck. All of the deckhands, passengers, and crew were below having dinner. Little did they know that it would be their last. Our first mate raised the black flag and fired off our cannons. The men below deck in the galleon came running above deck to find out what was going on.

"With a hand signal from Gaspar, we yelled out our war cry. The battle was on. We shot the first men as they came above deck. Right and left, they were falling like helpless babies who had never learned to walk. The next surge of men to come above were armed with swords and pistols. The real slaughter was about to begin. Men, women, and children were running, screaming. They all were desperately trying to hide from us. But there was no hiding. We were in control. The ship would soon be ours. Victory was within our reach. Sword fights broke out. You could hear the clanging of metal, followed by death cries everywhere.

"In less than two hours we took possession of the ship. We captured the captain and first mate and hanged both of them from the mast of the ship. The moon cast a sickly, pale glow over their dead bodies swinging in the wind. We rounded up all of the men who were still alive. We cut their throats before we pushed them overboard and fed them to the sharks. We tied the women together so we could take them to Captiva, where we would hold them for ransom.

"With the ship now under our control, we started rummaging through the hull for the treasure. In the cargo bay we found six chests full of gold, two full of diamonds, and three with emeralds. There were silks and linens. The finest treasure, however, were the six kegs of rum that we found stacked in a corner of the ship. The kegs of rum alone were enough to make the conquest worthwhile. In the galley we found an abundance of lavish food. There were pies and cakes, large rounds of beef, and twelve pigs ready to be roasted. What a feast we were to have that night.

"Our ship was soon loaded with the treasure, the rum, and the food. We turned our sails and set for Captiva. We set the galleon ablaze. The fire from the ship rose into the night sky and filled it with raging flame and smoke. The flames could be seen for miles and miles on the barren ocean. We always burned our captive ships after we finished ransacking them, just to make sure no one aboard was left alive.

"As we landed back onshore, there was shouting, singing, laughing, and dancing. This had been the most exciting and profitable victory in a long time. We unloaded the ship and buried most of the treasure deep in the sand at various locations on the island. There was so much food that night I didn't know where to begin. Rum was pouring freely and by midnight we were all filled with merriment and song.

"Gaspar stood up at one point and started singing, 'I am the Pirate King, it is, it is a glorious thing to be a Pirate King.'

"We all laughed until Hernando suddenly stood up and faced Gaspar. He had only been with the crew a short while and did not know how quick Gaspar's temper was. Hernando was very drunk and for a moment had taken leave of his senses.

"'Well, maybe you are a pirate king, but you can't get Josefa to give you the time of day, *(hiccup)* of day *(hiccup)*. What kind of king are you when you can't even get a pretty girl to smile at you? What good are you?' Hernando laughed and looked around to see if everyone else was joining in on the joke, but we were all deadly silent.

"Josefa was a tall, beautiful, sixteen-year-old Mexican princess Gaspar was holding for ransom. He loved her deeply but she did not return his affections. He showered her with beautiful clothing and jewels and made all the other women on the island serve as her handmaidens. Josefa was strong-willed. She hated Gaspar and would not speak to him when he came to call upon her.

"Hernando did not realize that no one on the crew ever spoke or joked about Josefa. Gaspar stared at him. The scar under his left eye glowed white against the red of his angry face. He gestured for Hernando to come forward. He continued to joke with Gaspar as he stumbled over.

"'Now, if you were as good-looking as Juan Carlos here, you might have a chance. But you are too old. Why, I understand that she reads poetry to him every night when you are asleep.'

"We all held our breath. Hernando did not realize the danger he was in. He was still laughing when Gaspar plunged a sword into his heart. He slumped over and was dead before he hit the ground.

"Gaspar then turned to Juan Carlos, his sword dripping red, and said, 'So, you like poetry, do you?' He aimed his pistol and shot Carlos between the eyes.

"We all huddled together and sat there silently. We didn't know where Gaspar's rage would turn next. He held his sword over his head and looked at Josefa's cottage. He ran to the door and tried to open it. The door was locked. With his pistol he blew it open. She was sitting at her dressing table combing her hair.

"When she saw Gaspar, she stood up. 'What do you want? You are not welcome here.'

"'Perhaps I'm not good enough for you,' Gaspar replied. 'Not good enough for you to read poetry to me.'

"'I don't know what you are talking about. Get out of here now!'

"Gaspar went over to her and grabbed her by the waist. He pulled her close. Her face turned red. She stared at the drunken man holding her. Hate poured out of her eyes. She looked at him and then spit in his face. In a moment of insane, angry passion, he ran the sharp edge of his sword through her neck. Her body fell lifelessly to the floor. He stood there for a moment, and when he realized what he had done, he let out a blood-curdling scream. He ran out to the ocean and fell, sobbing, on the sand.

"He had just killed the only woman he had ever truly loved. It was the only time in his life that he felt remorse for something he had done. He lay on the beach until the sun rose the next morning. His first mate, Daniel, was waiting for him.

"Gaspar motioned to him. 'I want the ship loaded by high noon. We are setting sail for Barbados.'

"'But, Captain, it will take days to prepare for such a long journey. How can we get ready by noon?'

"'Do as I say!'

"'Aye, aye, Captain.'

"Daniel knew better than to argue—Gaspar never gave an order twice.

"At once the men started to prepare the ship. We got shovels and dug up as much of the treasure as we could. Each chest weighed two thousand pounds. It took ten men just to lift them out of the sand. Our livestock and food were loaded into the cargo bay. The women hostages were tied up and put below deck. At noon, about half of the treasure had been loaded. We had to leave some of it behind because there just wasn't enough time to dig it all up.

"With most of the crew aboard ship, Gaspar and the officers burned all of the cabins and cottages to the ground. We left no trace of ever having been there. We set sail for Barbados with the *Gasprilla* loaded with gold, diamonds, and other treasures beyond belief. We left behind the isle of Captiva forever, the safe haven that had been our home for the past ten years. As we sailed away to new adventure, little did anyone aboard know that our life of piracy would be over in just a few short hours. It was a hot day and the sun was beating down on us. A few miles ahead, it looked like there was another ship in the distance. It was not too far away so Gaspar ordered the first mate to steer the ship a little closer. As it came into our sight, it appeared to be a British cargo ship. It was large and was probably carrying gold and silver.

"Gaspar looked at the ship and yelled, 'Full sail ahead, mates. Let's take them for all we can!'

"Arrogantly, Gaspar let up the black flag. He was going to attack without fear. We made quick time and were soon upon our prey. Gaspar stood on the bridge giving orders. Most of the men were tired and had no fight left. We didn't need the treasure. Our ship had a full load now. If we took on more cargo now, we would run the risk of sinking. But no one argued. We waited for the attack with little enthusiasm. We came upon the ship in broad daylight, but we had not been spotted, or so we thought. There was no one on deck. We should have known then that something was wrong. We pulled up beside the ship and prepared to board. All of a sudden, we could see the American flag being raised. Loud yells came from the other ship. The deck was soon swarming with soldiers. They pulled back canvas cloths and exposed large cannons. We could see now that this was not a cargo ship at all! It was an American warship. We saw the words USS *Enterprise*. But now it was too late. We had been fooled. Our fate was sealed. There was little chance of escaping. The *Enterprise* was large, powerful, and fast. Gaspar gave the command to pull away.

"We could hear the captain from the other ship, 'Attack and take no prisoners. Hang or shoot anyone in sight.'

"The *Gasprilla* desperately made an attempt to escape. *Boom, boom, boom*. They began to fire their cannons at our ship. We sailed straight ahead. Gunshots filled the air. *Boom, boom, boom*. The thunder of cannons screamed across the waters at us. The *Enterprise* was quickly gaining speed. Yells and shouts broke out on our ship. All of us were preparing to go to our deaths but not without a good fight first. *Boom, boom, boom*. Cannonballs were flying everywhere. Our ship was struck with a cannonball broadside, and we started to slow down. We were hit again, and the main sail came crashing down. We all but stopped. We were armed with guns, rifles, and swords—anything we could find. The *Enterprise* pulled up beside us and the soldiers boarded our ship. The men of our crew were being shot down three and four at a time. Half the men were dead within thirty minutes. Gaspar was standing high on the bridge above everyone else, the star-shaped scar burning white hot on his face. A navy officer came behind him and thrust his sword toward Gaspar. But he turned just in time and shot the man in the heart. Six more officers charged and surrounded him. He surveyed the ship and crew. Most of his men were dead, lying in pools of their own blood.

"We were slowly sinking, and a new surge of soldiers was boarding our decks. Gaspar wrapped the anchor chain around his waist, brandished his sword over his head, and yelled, 'You will never take me alive.' He screamed and then jumped into the shark-infested waters."

The pub was quiet now. Most of the sailors had gone home. The old man finished his story and then sat there silently without moving. The reporter was dazed by the story. He took a drink of warm ale, jotted down a few more notes, and pulled out the sack of gold.

"Well, I think that's quite a story. You know, legend has it that Gaspar swam back to shore."

The reporter laughed and looked over at the old man. He was slumped in his chair. Smith stood up and went over to him. "Hey, that's a great story. Were you really there, or did you hear this story from someone else?"

The old man didn't answer. The reporter shook his shoulder and saw that the old man wasn't breathing. He pulled back the hood that had been covering the old man's face. It was scarred and cut. Along his jaw-line, there were faded scars that looked like teeth marks. He held the candle up to the old man's lifeless face, and there under his left eye was a large scar in the shape of a five-pointed star. The reporter stared for a minute—could it really be? Was this old and bent man the King of Pirates? He thought to himself for a moment and then shook his head. He placed the gold in the dead man's lap and then disappeared into the dark, foggy night.

© 1996 Mitchell O'Rear
route66@romancingtheroadways.com

"The art of storytelling has given me insight into and understanding of the child's view of life and has inspired me to encourage all youth with whom I come into contact to carry on the tradition of our fathers and forefathers of sharing knowledge through stories. There is so much to tell and so little time and too much of the past that we will never know."

William Wiseman
Eustis

Bill Wiseman was born in Paterson, New Jersey. Early in his life, he moved to Florida, where he operated a fishing camp on the Ocklawaha River. Later Bill had a woodworking shop in Eustis, Florida. One could not find better neighbors than Bill and his wife, Stasia, who have now purchased the old Seven Roses Farm in Indiana to be closer to their only grandchild.

In his woodworking shop, Bill builds beautiful musical instruments of the past—dulcimers, psalteries, and zithers. He also makes a large number of ooonee cans, wonderful little instruments, as well as wooden ornaments. Bill is not only a good emcee but is often declared the "top entertainer" at the many festivals where he delights his audiences with his own style of music, stories, and humor.

Gramps' Chickens

In years past, many stories, jokes, and songs were written about hens and chickens. Back in the pioneer days on the farms and ranches, even in town, most everybody had chickens—raised them for food. I'd like to tell you a story my cousin PeeWee told me about his grandpa and the chickens that he raised.

Last year on the way back from Kentucky, I thought I'd go and visit cousin PeeWee out in the Panhandle. That's up in north Florida there, way up in northwest Florida, almost up to the Alabama border. I don't get up too often, but when I go up, many people call me "cousin." I'm not really their cousin—not anyone's except PeeWee's. Well, PeeWee had a grandpa who had a farm up there. They always called him "Gramps." Well, Gramps passed on and left the farm to PeeWee. I'm sure that some of you have heard me say that PeeWee was a lanky boy, like myself, but he grew up to be a giant of a man. Yet his family still called him PeeWee. After he got so big, it always got a chuckle from any strangers who happened to be around.

But anyway, PeeWee ran this farm. They had a nice pecan orchard and a couple of cows, and of course some chickens and a few other farm animals. We were going to go out on the back porch the evening I got there and play some music together with a few friends from around the area, PeeWee and myself. I was just getting my instrument out when I saw something go by—the strangest looking creature you ever saw—never saw anything like that in my life.

I said to PeeWee, "What was that?"

He said, "Oh! That's the last of the offspring of some of Gramps' experiments."

"What kind of experiments?" I asked.

"Well," he said, "as the story goes, Gramps used to raise these carrier pigeons, you know, the kind of pigeons that carry messages. They used a lot of them during World War One. They would go to the battlefields and carry these messages back and forth tied on their legs. Gramps got an idea to breed these carrier pigeons with woodpeckers. Yeah! It worked out real good because Gramps had the only carrier pigeons that ever went to deliver the message and knocked on the door. That was great! Being a scientific man, Gramps wanted to go on to bigger and better things."

"Is that right?" I said. "I didn't know your grandpa was a scientist."

"Oh, yeah," said PeeWee. "All he lacked being a full-fledged scientist was his education."

"I see," I said and kinda chuckled.

"Of course, while he had no formal education, he got most of his science learning from those popular science books and science fiction and even comic books. He wanted to experiment with interbreeding different kinds of chickens. He commenced to figure out a way, and he didn't do it the natural way. No! What he would do, he would take an egg from each one and make a tiny little hole in each end of the shell, and then he would blow the insides into a cup. He had some magic potion he would mix with that and stir it all up and get it mixed real good, and hopefully put half back in each egg."

"What was the results of this experiment?" I asked.

"Well, some of them worked out real good and some not so good. Some chickens he bred had four legs, and that was fine if you raised them on wire, because all the younguns could have a drumstick. But out here on the farm, some were real good and some not so good. The ones with the four legs, scratching towards each other, they'd just scratch and scratch and scratch and they'd dig a hole, and they would go down into the ground and, golly, you would have to reach down and pull them back up. If he left them overnight, they'd be gone—no telling where they went. But then on the other hand, the ones with the legs that were away from each other, they were okay because if they tried to run away, one would be going in one direction and one in the other direction and they were easy to catch. You didn't have to chase them—they hardly moved a bit. But the ones with four legs all going in the same direction, we never could catch them to see what they looked like. He lost money on them.

"Now, some of these chickens—of course, the way he'd mix the potion—some of them came out with two heads. That wasn't good, no, because they ate a lot and they kept getting bigger and bigger and no telling what was inside because, you see, there was no other end. They just kept eating and eating—took a lot of feed. But on the other hand, if one chicken had two heads, then the other one that hatched out, of course, it had two tails. That was good! Yeah! Didn't have to feed it. And it was shucking eggs out of both ends. Got plenty of eggs. Made lots of money off of those.

"And then there were the chickens that had two wings on one side. They were pretty good too, because they'd just fly around in a circle, around in a circle, around in a circle. He decorated some of them and sold them to the youngsters for pets. They were real good pets, and he made money off of those.

"Then he had one breed that had four wings—a great, big chicken. He bred that one with the carrier pigeon. That was good, because that was a great, big—the biggest carrier pigeon you could believe. Well, that carrier pigeon could carry little packages and deliver them back and forth.

"Now, some of them that had four wings didn't have any legs but that didn't bother Gramps a bit. He built this little trough, filled it with water right on down into the pond, and they would come scooting in and just land into that water trough and slide out into the pond and float out around there just like a duck. They were fine! He sold them to places that specialize in buffalo wings. So he did all right with those too.

"Now, I'm getting to a part that might be hard to believe. There was one breed of chicken that was born and just grew and grew. Didn't have any wings, didn't have a head nor a tail nor legs. It was just one great big mass of feathers laying there. Gramps wondered what to do with those, but he ended up making a lot of money off of them. He sold them to all these fast food places for chicken breast sandwiches. Got the biggest chicken breast sandwiches out of those you ever did see.

"Well, all good things must come to an end. Gramps passed on and took the secret with him. I guess it's just as well he did because the last thing that he tried, he took an alligator egg and mixed it with a buzzard egg, and that was the most gosh-awful looking creature you ever did see.

"And that's the tale of Gramps' chickens. Got your dulcimer tuned up? Let's play."

Man's Best Friend

As I grew up, I was a devotee of the old saw, "A dog is a man's best friend." Being a "dawg" man, having a cat as a pet never entered my mind. As a boy, we had hounds, beagles, and lots of other dogs. In later years when I had a family of my own, we had a dog, Snoopy. Snoopy lived to be about sixteen years old, and when he died, it was like losing a member of the family. The loss was so traumatic that we decided not to get another pet.

We are outdoor folks, and here in central Florida we spend a lot of time on the rivers and lakes. Early spring about eleven years ago, our daughters were canoeing on the Ocklawaha River. They found a little kitten on a tree branch that was hanging over the riverbank.

I wasn't surprised when our youngest daughter, Sheree, took this kitten to her home in Gainesville. Whenever I went to visit, the kitten would hide, as she would from all strangers. I really had never got a good look at the cat before Sheree called me one day and asked if I would take care of the kitten for two weeks while she moved.

Of course I was willing. I would do almost anything for my daughters. After all, two weeks is not that long! Would you believe, eight years later I still have the cat? Her name is Agatha Christie—Aggie for short.

Aggie and I made friends and understood each other almost from the beginning. She seemed to know that my home would be her home from that time forward.

I play the dulcimer. I like to practice out in back by the woodpile and do almost every evening. Aggie always comes, sits, and listens. I can make a mistake or play the same piece over and over, and she doesn't mind.

One evening when I was playing out by the woodpile with Aggie sitting close by, she suddenly jumped up and ran out to the open yard. I got up to see what was wrong. Usually I leave my dulcimer on the

arms of the chair when I take a break, but this time, in my haste to follow Aggie, I took the dulcimer with me. Not ten seconds after I left the
chair, there was a loud crash. A dead tree had fallen right where I had
been sitting. It flattened the chair to the ground.

Did Aggie have a premonition that something was going to happen,
or, with her keen ears, did she hear the moaning of the tree as it started to fall? Either way she lured me away from the danger and saved my
life.

Aggie now had the run of the place. When winter set in, Aggie
would slip into the house in the evening to be by the fireplace. I believe
she listened to the weather reports, because she seemed to know when
it was going to be a cold night.

Many nights I would fall asleep in the den by the fire with Aggie
sleeping on my stomach. One night Aggie jumped up and woke me
with a start. She was staring at the chimney. Sure enough, I heard a roar
coming from the fireplace.

I ran outside and saw fire and sparks shooting out over the roof. We
had a chimney fire. I couldn't spray the hose on it. That would cause it
to blow up. Fast as I could, I closed the flue and the fire went out. Again,
thanks to Aggie, another disaster was averted.

Aggie is older now, but she still loves to hear me play the dulcimer
out by the woodpile. She likes people but doesn't care for strange cats.
She tolerates and shares her food with a possum. She has developed a
little limp and a couple of allergies, but we're still buddies and I do take
good care of her, because she, a cat, is my best friend.

© 1995 William Wiseman

South Florida

Romantic and historic south Florida, with its unique Everglades, its coral reefs, Seminoles, and "Big Waters," is a greenhouse for storytellers. Tellers along Florida's east coast have large audiences and many opportunities to practice their art, yet even these seasoned tellers find it difficult to transfer this energy to the printed page. Tellers from both the east and west coasts, such as Peg Brown, Judy Gail, Charlotte Gomez-Lippincott, Melinda Munger, and Linda Spitzer, who took the time and effort to share their stories, have made a real contribution to the art. Their stories will bring pleasure to many who would never hear them in person. The three teachers in Sebring, who collaborated and gave us "Three Little Cracker Pigs;" Teresa Stein, who shared one of her many historical nuggets; and Judith Leipold, who has a true gift for creativity, have contributed stories that will enchant and enlighten readers and listeners for years to come.

—Annette J. Bruce

"Discovering storytelling marked a dramatic change in my life. Previously very shy about speaking in public, I found something magical happening when I began telling to audiences. Storytelling was, for me, that road less traveled that has made all the difference."

Peg Brown
Sarasota

Peg Brown was born in Montgomery, Alabama, and moved to the Sarasota, Florida, area in 1956. She was a media specialist in Sarasota County schools. She got her storytelling start by telling stories to her students, and after attending her first Florida Storytelling Camp around 1988 she started telling professionally. She is looking forward to becoming a full-time storyteller now that she has retired.

The Legend of Lake Okeechobee

The following is my adaptation of a Native American legend. I have encountered at least two other versions of the Lake Okeechobee legend—one I heard a number of years ago from the Native American legend-keeper, Jackalene Crow, and the other one is Betty Mae Jumper's story "Two Hunters," which appears in Legends of the Seminoles *(Pineapple Press, 1994). I imagine that since it is a cautionary tale on a subject dear to the hearts of mothers the world over, it has been told in many versions.*

North of the Everglades in south Florida, there is a large, shallow lake called Okeechobee. It has been there a long, long time, but the Seminoles say it has not always been there. Once, they say, in a village on the edge of the Everglades, lived two brothers. They were growing up to be skillful hunters, and they always hunted together. They hunted the deer, the bear, and many other wild creatures and kept not only their family but much of their village supplied with meat. They were never known to come home from the hunt empty-handed.

But then there came a day when they were not successful in their hunting. They traveled all that day, further north than they usually went from their home. That night they made camp, and in the morning they continued north, but again they found no game. As the day went on, they noticed the sky was beginning to darken, and the air felt strangely heavy. Thunder rolled and lightning began to flash across the sky. Loud cracks sounded around them, and the air was filled with an acrid, burning smell from the strikes. Neither brother could remember ever having been in the midst of such a storm, and they were frightened. At last, they found refuge in the hollow trunk of a huge dead tree. During the night, they got little sleep as the storm crashed about them. They ate the last of the food they carried with them, and when they woke the next morning they were hungry and thirsty.

The older brother went out first to look around. Soon he called excitedly, "Come and see what I have found!" When the younger brother crawled out of the tree trunk, he found his older brother holding up, by their gills, two strange-looking fish. "Look what I have found—two beautiful bass."

"But how did you catch them so quickly?" The younger brother asked. "I have seen no water nearby."

"I found them swimming in a pool of water in that big hollow stump over there. Somehow they must have been caught up in that great storm and have come down with the rain. Start a fire, and we will cook ourselves a fine meal."

The younger brother was reluctant. "No, I do not think we should eat these fish. It is not natural that they should have been in such a place, and, besides, I do not believe they are bass. They look so pale and their scales shine strangely. You know that our mother has often warned us not to eat things we do not recognize."

But the older brother was thinking only with his stomach. He built a fire and cooked the fish, and, because his younger brother would not touch them, he ate every bit of them, licking his fingers and teasing his brother about the fine meal he was missing because he was scared by their mother's old tales.

They set out hunting again, but after a time the older brother started to feel strange. His arms began to itch, and gradually the itch spread all over his body. Soon he was lagging behind. When the younger brother noticed this and turned back, he found his sibling staring in horror at his arms. The young man called out, "Brother, what is wrong?"

"It was those strange fish. You were right. I should never have eaten them. Look! See the scales on my arms, my body. My legs are beginning to join together. I think I am turning into a snake." The younger brother started toward him, but he cried, "Stay back. You must leave me. Go home and get our mother and the other elders. Perhaps they will know what to do."

The younger brother turned and ran back toward their village. He traveled as fast as he could, not stopping to eat or drink. When he reached the village and told his strange story, his mother and many others followed him back. At moonrise the next night, they reached the spot where he had left his brother. They called out the young man's name, but for a time they heard nothing. Then the bushes began to tremble, and in the moonlight they saw the head of a great, pale snake rise among the trees.

The snake spoke slowly. "It is me. Listen while I still have the power of speech. I should have heeded your warnings, oh, my mother, my brother, but I chose to go against the ancient laws of our people when I ate the strange fish. Now it is too late for you to help me. Already I am forgetting what I was and becoming this snake in mind as well as body."

When his family tried to come closer to comfort him, he cried out, "Stay back. Do not approach me now for I do not know what this thing I have become might do to you. I must leave you before I do you some harm."

The snake turned and began to crawl away, and as the people followed from a distance, they saw that he was growing even larger. The brush and trees bent beneath his weight, and a great trench was gouged into the ground by his passing. A light rain began to fall. At last the huge snake stopped and began to coil around and around with great speed. The rain was a torrent now, and the people lost sight of him. When the rain stopped at last, before them the people saw a great, shallow lake. From its midst, the head of the pale snake rose. In a voice more of a hiss than human speech, it called out, "Do not forget me!" Then it sank beneath the water and was never seen by the people again.

The Seminoles say that the trench carved by the snake's great body became the Kissimmee River and the lake it made is Lake Okeechobee. Seminole mothers still tell their children the story of the unfortunate young warrior as a warning to be careful what they eat.

© 1996 Peg Brown

"As teachers, we realize a story well told has a powerful impact on today's children. The exposure to cultural history in this simplistic form allows the children to enjoy and develop a new appreciation for a Cracker's heritage."

Kim Douberley, LaNita Roth, & Alice Taylor
Sebring

Kim, LaNita, and Alice are three Southern belles who have collaborated to produce still another version of one of our childhood favorites. Kim and Alice were born in Avon Park, Florida, and LaNita was born in Sparta, Tennessee. All three earned bachelor's degrees in Elementary Education in a Florida university or college.

Kim, LaNita, and Alice became friends while teaching fourth grade at Sun 'n Lake Elementary School in Sebring, Florida. Their enjoyment of Florida history in conjunction with their Cracker heritage inspired them to blend the colorful expressions of their extended families with a commonly known children's tale. Kim, LaNita, and Alice are all married, and Kim has two children.

Three Little Cracker Pigs

Not long ago, near the south end of Florida's center ridge, lived a family of piney-woods rooters—Mama Rooter and her three little piglets, Flossie, Bubba, and Flo. They were a happy family, but their shack was becoming increasingly crowded as all their waistlines expanded from feasting on Mama's grits, biscuits, sausage gravy, and lemonade.

Even though Mama knew it was time to send her oldest piglet, Flossie, out across the land to seek her fortune, she enjoyed having her around so much that she put off doing it. One morning when Flossie and Bubba got stuck in the doorway, both trying to be first for Mama's sausage gravy and grits, Mama decided it was time to send Flossie out to make it on her own. She packed her a basket of sour orange jelly, corn pone, and collard greens. Flossie was excited about her new adventure. She took the basket and headed out.

Mama stopped her to offer a last piece of advice. "Flossie, 'member when you are chasin' yore dream, always go whole-hog, but don't you be a-forgettin' yore manners."

Flossie was snorting loudly when she arrived at the edge of the hammock. Here, paths crisscrossed and went in every direction, so she had to make her first decision. She was glad she could read the signpost, and when she saw "north" on it, she remembered how the Northern tourists were always talking about how wonderful everything was where they came from. She had no trouble at all making up her mind. She headed north!

Flossie ambled along, enjoying the scenery, until she came upon what appeared to be an enormous green carpet. The sweet smell of freshly mowed grass enticed Flossie to stay around for a while. She put down her basket and built herself a cool, sod house. Pleased with her efforts, she sat down to admire her work. It was then that she realized how hungry she was. Under a nearby shade tree, she spread her blanket for a picnic.

As she finished her last swallow of sour orange jelly, her ears picked up a strange voice: "Fore!" A small white ball suddenly came from nowhere and landed—*kerplunk*—in her mason jar of lemonade.

Flossie looked around, trying to find where the voice and ball had come from, and she saw four strange-looking creatures coming over the hill. Each one carried a bag of clubs. Flossie quickly grabbed up her basket and hid down by the lake. From behind the cattails, she spotted a gator sunning himself on the shore. Remembering her best manners, Flossie politely offered him the remainder of her corn pone dinner.

The mean, ole, snaggle-toothed gator quickly accepted. But instead of corn pone, he had a king-size pork sandwich for lunch.

"My, what a delicious whole-hog dinner that was!" said the mean, ole, snaggle-toothed gator as he snorted, slapped his tail, and slid back into the lake.

Several weeks passed, and Mama Rooter realized her two remaining piglets had grown quite portly when Bubba and Flo would not fit in the washtub for their weekly bath.

She packed Bubba a lunch box of dumplings, cowpeas, fried green tomatoes, and mint tea. She offered her only son this sage bit of wisdom. "Don't ever go off half-cocked and always 'member yore manners."

Bubba was feeling adventurous because he was free of Mama's apron strings for the first time in his young life. Shortly he arrived at the edge of the hammock. Bubba perused the words on the signpost beside the wandering trails. He wasn't sure what all the words were, but he read the word "west" and decided to go in the direction that arrow was pointing because he had always wanted to be a cowboy. Moseying along, Bubba did not travel many miles the first day.

He got a late start on the second day, but soon the trail carried him past a barbed-wire fence, where he spotted a cow hunter rounding up cattle in a pasture. Roping and branding the cattle looked like fun so he decided this was where he wanted to build his ranch house. When the Cracker stopped and sat down beside the fire to have a cup of ole Joe, bold Bubba sauntered up beside him and, with admiration written all over his face, asked if he was a real cowboy.

The cow hunter smiled and replied, "Yore lookin' at the real McCoy!"

Bubba felt right at home and asked if he might use some of the fenceposts and barbed wire to build himself a home.

"Hep yoreself, youngun," replied the cow hunter. Bubba scouted around for a good site near shade and water for his "spread." Nearby, a watering hole and live oak tree provided the perfect place. After great effort, the exhausted little pig was quite satisfied with his Cracker shack—the ranch-style house and spread would have to come later.

He sat down under the oak tree to enjoy his noon meal. As he sipped the refreshing mint tea, he spotted a gator sunning himself on the bank.

Remembering what his Mama taught him, he hollered, "Mister, want summa my tea?"

The surly, ole, shifty-eyed gator quickly accepted, but it wasn't tea he was really after. Instead of mint tea, the gator had pork chops for dinner.

"My, what a delicious whole-hog dinner that was!" said the surly, ole, shifty-eyed gator as he snorted, slapped his tail, and slid back into the watering hole.

Mama Rooter hadn't heard from her piglets in a month of Sundays and was leery of sending her youngest piglet out to seek her fortune. But Flo was an inquisitive youngster and pleaded with her Mama to let her find her own way in the world.

Mama Rooter said, "Jumpin' Jehoshaphat, child! Why would you want to do that?"

Flo replied, "Please, Mama, I'll remember to use my manners and to look before I leap."

Hesitantly, Mama Rooter packed a dinner bucket of chicken pilau, swamp cabbage, fried okra, watermelon, and blackberry tea for her little darlin'. As Flo headed out of the hammock, Mama called after her, "Remember your upbringin' and use yore common sense."

Before long, Flo found herself at the signpost on the outskirts of the hammock. Remembering yarns spun by great-grandfather Rooter about the legendary Seminole Indians, Flo headed south toward the Everglades. Flo walked and walked until her little piggy hooves were sore and tired. She spied a dugout canoe in a nearby branch and with it traveled deeper into the river of grass. She spotted a wisp of smoke rising from a nearby island and maneuvered the canoe onto shore. A Seminole woman was cooking sofkee on an open fire near a chickee.

Flo approached the woman and politely said, "Pardon me, ma'am, could you kindly tell me how I might go 'bout buildin' me a house like that un?"

The kindly Seminole replied, "You must always use strong timber and green palmetto fronds."

Flo discovered a small clearing not far from the Seminole village and set to work constructing a sturdy little chickee. When she finished the chickee, she went to the water's edge to wash her hands and face and came snout to snout with a wily, ole, weak-chinned gator.

Using her common sense as well as her manners, Flo said, "Won't you please join me this evenin' for supper?"

The wily, ole, weak-chinned gator hadn't had a decent meal in a blue moon. He replied, "Why, thank you, missy. I'd be right honored to eat supper with you." He swam away drooling over the country ham and red-eye gravy he was going to enjoy as his next meal.

Flo saw the menacing glint in his eye, and, quick as greased lightning, she trotted to the Seminole village to ask for help. She saw the same Seminole woman stoking the fire. "Pardon me, ma'am, I was wonderin' if you could hep me with a small problem. I've invited that wily, ole, weak-chinned gator to supper and I b'lieve he intends to eat me. Is there someone who could give me a hand?"

The wise old Seminole woman stirred the sofkee in the pot and replied, "My son is very good at wrestling gators, and I'm sure he could help you."

The woman's son accompanied Flo back to the little chickee. When the wily, ole, weak-chinned gator arrived for supper, the young warrior wrestled him to the ground and securely tied his jaws shut.

Shortly thereafter, the Seminole family and Flo sat down to a delicious meal of gator tail, swamp cabbage, fried okra, watermelon, and blackberry tea. Flo enjoyed herself so much she decided to settle permanently in this clearing of the Everglades.

Some weeks later, the young warrior gave Flo an alligator purse and matching shoes.

Moral: Use common sense, and don't feed the gators!

© Kim Douberley, LaNita Roth, & Alice Taylor
cddouber@strato.net (Kim Douberley)
lanitaroth@yahoo.com (LaNita Roth)

"I have followed my childhood dream of being the wandering minstrel, knowing that every word I speak and song I sing has the power to touch the lives of those listening and to tap the innate wonder that lies within each one of us about the universe and all of life's creatures."

Judy Gail
Miami

Storyteller, balladeer, and author Judy Gail was born in Hartford, Connecticut, but has made Miami her home since 1983. She is a performer for the Florida Humanities Council Speakers Bureau, impersonating Florida pioneer Mary Barr Munroe and presenting "The History of Work and Labor in Story and Song." Judy wrote, produced, and narrated the WLRN/Dade County Board of Education four-part documentary, "AIDS: The Plague of Our Times," which was aimed at high school students and won Best Bets in the *Miami Herald*. She created and produced the NBC fundraising special "Hurricane at the Zoo" to help rebuild Miami MetroZoo after Hurricane Andrew. Her first book, *Day of the Moon Shadow: Tales with Ancient Answers to Scientific Questions*, was a Prestigious Awards winner in 1996. *Work and Labor: A History in Story and Song,* Judy's second book, was published in 1998. Included in *Storytellers: A Biographical Directory of 120 Entertainers Worldwide,* Judy performs both nationally and internationally.

The Great Florida Alligator Conjure Man

This is the story of the great Florida Alligator Conjure Man. His name was Brother Monday. He was named Brother Monday 'cause he was born in Africa, and in his tribe they named the children after the day they was born on. Well, they also called him Brother Monday 'cause he had as much energy on Monday as he did on Tuesday, Wednesday, Thursday, Friday, Saturday, and Sunday! Now, Brother Monday had special gifts. He was a conjure man—like a medicine man and a magician all in one! He could talk to the animals. Why, he could talk to the crocodiles. He could talk to that dangerous water horse called the hippopotamus. He could talk to the king of the beasts, the lion. Brother Monday loved the animals, and they loved him.

Now, a terrible thing happened to Brother Monday. He was captured, put in chains, thrown on a boat, and taken across the ocean, where he was sold as a slave to a master in the state of Georgia. Brother Monday couldn't stand bein' a slave, and he decided to escape! It was real dangerous, and he had to conjure and conjure and conjure up all kinds of spells to get the scent off himself and keep those hound dogs from findin' him. But he managed to escape and run and run and run and run till he came all the way to the southern tip of Florida, in what today is Dade County in Miami. There he lived with the Seminole Indians like he was their brother and they were his.

The Seminoles loved Brother Monday. He taught 'em how to wrestle alligators and bring 'em back live to camp for fresh meat, and how to rub that gator fat all over 'emselves to keep those pesky mosquitoes away. Why, he showed 'em how to pull out saw grass—yes, he did—in order to get its tuberlike root. He taught 'em how to pound that root into flour, and cook it, and eat it, and roast it like a p'tata.

But, most important, Brother Monday could conjure. And he conjured up the future, and he saw the U.S. government was gonna break a treaty with those Seminole Indians and try to take over their land in southern Florida. And he said to his Indian brothers and sisters, "We gotta get ready. We gotta prepare. We gotta fight!" And they did—and they won! And that happened once. And that happened twice. And that happened three times. And that happened *four* times.

And after the fourth time, Brother Monday said, "I have a vision! I conjure the future. . . . I conjure the future. I conjure . . . I see there's gonna be another battle . . . and we'll lose *if we stay here!* We gotta pack ev'rythin' up, and we gotta go to the north central part of the state. We gotta go. Yes, we gotta go . . . to . . . to . . . Maitland Lake! There we will fight a battle, and we'll half lose . . . we'll lose the battle . . . but we won't lose the land! We'll have land to live on!"

Believe me, they packed up. Those Seminoles trusted Brother Monday. He'd been right ev'ry time before. So they all went up to Maitland Lake and there, just as Brother Monday had conjured, it happened. Terrible battle! But the Seminoles could stay on the land, and they're there today!

After that battle, when they all settled down again, Brother Monday said, "My time with you is up. I've done all I can do for you. It's time for me to leave."

The Seminoles were very sad. They loved Brother Monday like he was one of their own. But they understood. If a conjure man says it's time to go, then it's time to go! So, they made a big celebration feast for him. That night you could hear the Seminoles beatin' on their drums. You could smell alligator meat a-roastin'. Swamp deer too. Everyone was chantin' and singin' and dancin', 'specially Brother Monday. Why, he loved to dance, and he was singin' a song that went:

Alli alli alli alli alli alli alli wah!
Alli alli alli alli alli alli alli wah!

And there, right before ev'ryone's eyes—so help me, what I tell you is true—Brother Monday's right eye moves over to the right side of his face. His left eye moves over to the left side of his face. And his face grows longer and longer and longer. His arms and his legs grow shorter and shorter, and they get clawlike paws on the ends. His body grows longer and longer and longer, and he gets a tail that he whips back and forth. His skin turns scaly and green. Yes! Right in front of their eyes, Brother Monday turns into an *alligator!* His song turns into bellows. Yes! He starts bellowin' like the alligators.

Alli alli alli alli alli alli alli wah!

Alli alli alli alli alli alli alli wah!

And believe what I tell you now! All across Maitland Lake came every alligator that lived in the region. They filled up that lake from east to west and north to south. And there goes Brother Monday walkin' out right over each and ev'ry one of 'em! He walks on one. He bellows. They all bellow with him. He walks on two. He bellows. They all bellow with him. And you can bellow along too!

Alli alli alli alli alli alli alli wah!

Alli alli alli alli alli alli alli wah!

And then, he gets to the last alligator across that lake and—*it all stops!* Brother Monday sinks right into that lake, and ev'ry darned alligator sinks right into the lake along with Brother Monday. And it's more silent than silence has ever been in those parts!

Well, the story goes that ev'ry time there are people who need help, Brother Monday comes back from the alligators and helps them. Why, story goes that when them alligators were so badly poached for their skins to make pocketbooks, shoes, upholst'ry for furniture, and belts to wear, turnin' them gators into an endangered species, Brother Monday came back as a man and worked with them politicians to change the laws and protect them gators! And story goes that whenever you hear the alligators—all, all, all a-bellowin', all of 'em, yes, across the whole of Maitland Lake—and whenever you hear them gators bellowin'—all, all, all a-bellowin', all of 'em, yes, across whatever's left of them Florida Everglades—you know that Brother Monday's finished doin' another good deed for some folks or some needy critters. And then you know that it's time for him to go back and live with the alligators!

And that's the tale of Brother Monday.

Why the Woodpecker Has No Song

Music and Lyrics
Judy Gail

Inspired by an Old Florida folktale

judygailstories@cs.com

Sandspun

"My earliest recollection of story-telling was in my grandmother's kitchen listening to family stories."

Judith Leipold
Arcadia

Judith Leipold was born in New York and raised in a rural eastern Long Island community situated along the Connetquot River. She moved to Florida in 1973 and soon earned her "Cracker citizenship." Judith continued her education in librarianship and worked as a park ranger at Myakka River State Park. It was in this venue that she developed an appreciation for Florida natives, including plants, animals, and the human species. It was also here that she became reacquainted with storytelling. In 1988, she cofounded a tandem team known as Imagine That! Storytellers. As a member from 1990 to 1995, she performed throughout the state, including at the Stephen Foster Storytelling Festival and the Florida Storytelling Camp.

Today, Judith is employed as a school media specialist for Charlotte County public schools. She enjoys her hobbies of vegetarian cooking, organic gardening, and tale-telling to her five grandchildren.

Kissimmee Sam

Jacob Summerlin was one of Florida's most famous pioneers. They even say he was the first white child born in the Florida territory after it was ceded to the United States and that he grew up to be one of the most famous cattle ranchers in the history of our state.

Now, Jacob had a partner. They called him Kissimmee Sam. What? You say you've never heard of Sam? Then listen up because today I'm going to tell you about Sam's place in Florida history.

You see, Sam was a little tyke when his ma and pa came down to the Florida territory. That was about 1821. They came down in an ox-drawn wagon from one of the Carolinas, bringing all their cattle with them. As they were crossing the Kissimmee River, Sam got a notion to do some fishin'. The problem was he didn't have a pole nor nothing to bait it with. He was just leaning out of the back of the wagon, looking down in the river and letting his shirttail dangle in the water. All of a sudden, a big catfish came along and grabbed ahold of his shirt and pulled him right out of the wagon!

That fish was so big and strong that it would have pulled Sam all the way to Lake Okeechobee if it weren't for a she-panther. That mama panther had gone down to the river for a drink, and when she saw Sam bobbin' by, she reached out and grabbed him by the britches and pulled him to shore. I have to admit that's rather unusual behavior for any wild animal, 'specially a critter that craves solitude as much as a panther. Maybe Sam was just such a sight that she had to pull him out to figure out what was going on. Or maybe she was actually tryin' ter ketch that catfish. But I like to think it was because she had just lost one of her cubs and thought this youngun would be good company for the other one.

That mama panther raised Sam right 'longside her own cub, and he turned out as wild as any wildcat in the flatwoods. He could run like a weasel, out-wrestle a black bear, and climb a tree faster than a fox squirrel.

The day Sam met Jake Summerlin, Sam was out huntin' somethin' to eat when he heard Jake comin'. There was no time to skedaddle so he climbed up to the top of a cypress tree and tried to hide.

Now, Jake was jest a youngster himself, but he wus sharp. He looked up and asked, "Whatcha mean, sittin' up top of this here tree, with nothin' on atall?"

Sam had grown out of his britches long ago, so sure enough he was sittin' up top of that tree buck naked. Sam bared his teeth and snarled at Jake below.

"Boy, are you crazy or somethin'?" Jake demanded.

It wasn't the "crazy" part but the word "boy" that jerked Sam's head. "Who ya callin' 'boy'? I ain't no boy. I'm a panther."

"Horsefeathers! You ain't no panther. If you're a panther, where's yur tail?"

Sam turned 'round and saw that Jake was right. He didn't have one. That's when Sam figured he'd better climb down and make amends. Well, the years passed and Kissimmee Sam and Jake Summerlin became good friends. Sam was never exactly sure what he was. He just knew what he wasn't! He was no panther.

One time Sam and Jake were out in the marsh when out of nowhere came the biggest, meanest gator you've ever seen. I mean, he could've swallered a whole ox. He had his sights set right on skinny little Jake. Just as that gator opened up his mouth to bite down on Jake, Sam (fast as he was and all) jumped into the river and started to wrestle with that creature. They wrestled so-o-o hard that the water tilted the land this-a-way and that-a-way and ever which-a-way! But when everything finally settled down and the water got calm, Sam stood up. And I want ya ter know, there wasn't a scratch on him. But that gator? Pshew! There was nothin' left of him at all, 'ceptin' his tail. Sam looked at that tail and thought it might come in handy for somethin'. So he rolled it up and put it in his pack for later.

Sam and Jake went into business together. They started small with just a few of them old-timey scrub cows. Those cows were so bony, you could hang your hat on either one of their hipbones. You see, cattle had to find grass where they could, but with all those palmetters and wire-grass, it wasn't always so easy. Sam and Jake figured that if they could just burn off that tough, old prairie grass, what would come back was sure to be nice and tender. But they just weren't sure how they were going to get things fired up.

That's when Sam had an idea. He recollected seein' lightnin' and hearin' thunder as a baby up in Carolina. Back in those days, Florida hadn't 'come a state yet, so it didn't have any lightnin' of its own. So he took out that old gator tail he'd been savin' and started to whip it 'round his head and then he just let it crack! It sounded like the loudest crack of thunder you ever heard. Could of fooled anybody—even you! In fact, it must've fooled the sky itself 'cause as soon as the sky heard that whip a crackin', it sent the biggest bolt of lightnin' out of some clouds. Then it follered with another bolt and another! Every place the lightnin' struck, it left a puff of smoke, and every one of those puffs started to grow until all you could see was a blanket of fire just creepin' across that prairie.

Well, after all those palmetters and wiregrass burned, tender shoots started comin' up all over. Those cattle started eatin' and eatin' until Jake and Sam ended up with the fattest, purtiest cattle in Florida. Cowmen from the Panhandle to the Big Cypress began askin' Sam, "How 'bout comin' over our way and bringin' that gator tail whip and some of that lightnin' with ya?"

And you know, before you knew it, lightnin' was crackin' all over Florida, greenin' up the flatwoods and prairies for critters to munch on. That's when Kissimmee Sam figured out exactly what he was. He was the first Florida Cracker!

Imagine that!

© Judith Leipold
bookbubbe@aol.com

"Storytelling is a multi-purpose gift. It may be used not only for entertainment and teaching, but also for healing, loving, making peace, and opening doors to people of every race, religion, culture, and background. It has shaped and enriched my own life since early childhood, when I sat with my grandmother in the front porch swing listening to her stories."

Charlotte Gomez-Lippincott
Alva

Charlotte Gomez-Lippincott is a rare creature indeed—she was born in Ft. Myers, Florida, and is a lifelong resident of the Sunshine State. A fifth-generation southwest Florida native, Charlotte graduated from Florida Southern College and received her master's degree from the University of South Florida. She lives in Alva and teaches sixth grade at Alva Middle School. She has told stories since childhood and integrates storytelling into her daily life, sharing her love of storytelling with her students, colleagues, and listeners at various festivals and events in her community and throughout Florida.

The Gifts

I was born and raised in Alva, a small community in southwest Florida, where our lives revolved around family, church, and neighbors. In the community, there were one school, grades one through twelve, and two churches. I attended the Methodist church, with the purple-stained glass windows, the big bell, and a parsonage across the street from the church building. In a time when many homes were built flat on the ground with outhouses, our parsonage was built up off the ground with tall eaves, a screen porch, and indoor plumbing. Mrs. Cutshall's grown children bought and moved the old parsonage three lots down the street, and Mrs. Cutshall moved in.

Mrs. Cutshall came to Alva with her husband and children, hoping for a better life. She had raised the children in rural Mississippi during the Depression, and after moving to Alva, her husband was killed in a tragic sawmill accident. She was a tall, gentle woman whose smile made you feel special. At the post office, she gave me a hug and a smile. When I saw her at school, working in the cafeteria, she always smiled and waved, which made me feel like the most important kid in school. Sundays she was never too busy with the grown-ups at church to smile and greet me. Her smile radiated love.

Mrs. Cutshall was our youth group leader. She faithfully met with us each Sunday night. We studied, laughed, and had a great time. But each summer my cousin Eunice led our group while Mrs. Cutshall traveled with area youth to Connecticut to work in the tobacco fields. About the second summer Mrs. Cutshall was in her old parsonage home, we decided that we would surprise her and paint it while she was gone.

Eunice got the paint, brushes, sawhorses, and boards. Each morning, the whole gang met at Mrs. Cutshall's instead of at the river, where we usually spent our summer mornings. Even though the river was the only entertainment available to us, the painting had to be done in the morning, because it rained every afternoon.

My daddy said, "You must scrape the old paint off first. Get a smooth, clean surface before you start, or you won't have a good job when you finish."

The work was not exactly what we had expected. We used our hands to rub off the chipped paint and got splinters for our efforts. We had no ladders, so scaffolds had to be built, taken down, moved, and rebuilt. Working in the hot, summer sun in Florida was not anything like playing at the river. The humidity was high, and the tan index was well above ten. Our noses burned, and each day we went home for lunch as wet as if we had been swimming. We thought it would take a day or two at the most and we would be back in the cool water of the Caloosahatchee River. As two days stretched into four, we determined that, for Mrs. Cutshall, we would finish the job, no matter how long it took.

Of course, it was not all work. As children do, we laughed a lot as we shared and played jokes on each other. Short games of chase erupted as we splattered each other with paint. Our parents complained that we must be getting more paint on ourselves than on the house.

I remember coming around the back corner of the house and marveling at a large red hibiscus bloom. I wondered how Mrs. Cutshall was able to grow such beautiful plants. I lived two doors down, and we grew only sandspurs in the sugar-sand soil. But I had little time to reflect on the aesthetic beauty of God's creations—I had painting to do.

When we finished, we were so proud! We anxiously awaited the end of summer when Mrs. Cutshall would see her beautiful, sparkling white house. When she finally came home, she was overjoyed. Her smile was brighter than we ever remembered it, and she thanked us over and over again. How good we felt.

That was the impression I had as a child. As an adult, I can tell you that it didn't happen quite that way.

Among her material possessions, Mrs. Cutshall valued most her home and plants. That summer, her yard was not the beautiful tropical paradise it is today, but she had made a good start. After only two years, she had already planted young oaks that were as tall as we were, shrubs to start a hedge, flowers to attract butterflies, vines to wind up into the trees, and there was color everywhere. However, as youth, we were oblivious to the labor of love that had gone into the beauty that surrounded us. In our youthful exuberance and innocence, we stomped, broke, bruised, trampled, uprooted, painted, or otherwise destroyed anything that dared to grow within ten feet of where we were working.

Not only did we destroy her beautiful plants, Mrs. Cutshall's house became what she would later refer to as a "halfway house." Without ladders, we were unable to reach all the way to the top of the tall eaves, and so her beautiful, sparkling white house was white only part of the way up. It is hard to imagine the disappointment she must have felt when she returned and saw what we had done to her house and her precious plants. But I am convinced that no hint of this ever crossed her lips. She saw the givers instead of the gift and accepted our gift in the spirit in which it was given.

Many of the members of our youth group have moved away now. Sometimes one of them comes home to visit and comes to church to find Mrs. Cutshall. Invariably someone will ask, "Mrs. Cutshall, remember when we painted your house?" Her smile grows big as she laughs and hugs us and once again makes us feel special.

The gift we gave that summer flaked and peeled and has been redone several times over the years. But the gifts Mrs. Cutshall gave us—her love, her smile, her thoughtfulness, herself—will live on in our lives and in the lives of everyone with whom we share those gifts.

"Stories are the most direct route to understanding I know of. Whether you are trying to know a culture, a religion, an individual, the audience, or the teller, their story, properly listened to, throws the doors wide open."

Melinda Munger
Miami

Melinda Munger has been telling stories for twenty-two years. For the past twelve of those years, she has been the manager of the Imagination Factory, a storytelling outreach program of the Miami-Dade Public Library System that has served audiences of over a million in schools and at parks, camps, festivals, and other organizations.

During the past fifteen years, Melinda has performed and presented workshops at many venues, including the Stephen Foster, Cracker, and Ocala Storytelling Festivals, the Okefenokee and Spirit of the Suwannee Story Fests, the Florida Storytelling Camp, Vizcaya, the Miami Art Museum, the Dade Reading Council, F.A.M.E., the Florida Library Association, and the Hendry County In-Service Day.

Melinda lives in Miami. In her spare time, she learns and teaches Tai Chi.

No Mockingbirds on Friday

A while back, in the south part of Florida, there lived a mean man. He was about the orneriest old coot there ever was. He lived alone way out in the Everglades. He pretty much had to. You see, he was so cussed that he couldn't be around other people without fussing and fighting with them. He would come into town once every month or two, and, sure as you're born, by sundown he would be in some kind of fracas with somebody or other and the day would end with the sheriff escorting him to the edge of town and telling him his welcome was worn out for a while.

But there is almost nobody on this earth who is all bad. Every person has some little bit of goodness in him, some tender spot, and so did this old man. You see, he loved birds. All kinds of birds, but his special favorites were the mockingbirds. When those boy mockingbirds got to singing all night in the spring trying to find girlfriends, well, that sad song went straight to his crusty old heart. He said it was because they were feisty like himself, but that wasn't the truth. It was that sad, old, I-ain't-got-a-girlfriend song.

So, out of whatever goodness he had, the old man looked out for the mockingbirds. He would feed them, fix their broken wings, and put their babies back up into the nest when they fell. The mockingbirds became so trustful of the old man they would hop up and take food right from his hand. It is not easy to make friends with a mockingbird like that, but when you do, you have a friend for life—and then some.

One day the old man went into town and got up to his usual tricks. But this time he picked the wrong fight. Guns came into play, and, in a lizard's blink, that old fella was on his way to a place that was hotter than Orlando in August. It is sad to say, but nobody much cared. They figured he had gotten pretty much what he had asked for. Nobody missed him, that's for sure, except the birds. When the mockingbirds heard what had happened to their friend, they were heartbroken and mad! They did not think it was one bit fair, and, being feisty critters, like I said, they decided to do something about it.

The youngsters were all for charging in and just pulling their friend out. Older, wiser birds said it might not be that easy, but you know younguns. You can't tell them anything. They all got together and in no time were streaking low and fast through the flames and fumes of Hell. They were bold. They were determined. And more than a couple of them were humming the theme music from *Mission Impossible* as they flew. They found their friend hunkered down in a bonfire. Lining their target up along their beaks, they swooped in, grabbed him in thousands of tiny talons, and yanked, only to discover that he was chained down. Flying back to the rest of the flock nursing thousands of tiny hernias, they were ready to listen to Plan B.

Plan B was sensible enough. If you can't pull your friend out of the fire, put out the fire around him. Soon every mockingbird in Florida was flapping through Hell, determined to spit that fire out. However, while Hell is as hot as Orlando, it is not nearly as humid and it has almost twice as many sulfur fumes. By the time they reached the old man, they didn't have enough spit amongst them to put out a match.

Plan C was for each bird to fly in with a beak full of water. I believe you can guess what happened. Yep, they swallowed.

Plan D, however, was a keeper. This time they all flew out to the white beaches along Florida's coast, and each scooped up a beak full of sand. It worked like a charm. Soon the fire was out, the old man was (relatively) cool, and the birds were free to get back to the business of song-singing, nest-building, egg-laying, and youngun-feeding, which they had badly neglected through all this.

However, the Devil is nothing if not a good administrator. He doesn't just start those flames a-licking, then wander off and forget about it. No! Hell is a big, international concern. The Devil has orders and invoices and a boss to answer to. He makes daily rounds. When his next tour took him past the mockingbird's friend, he was pretty upset to see the fire put out. He demanded to know what had happened, but the old man just shrugged. He was mean, but he was not stupid. So the Devil just had the flames stoked up again.

When the mockingbirds heard, they went straight back to the beaches, scooped up more sand, and again smothered the fire. The next day the Devil was furious! He jumped up and down, stomped his hoof, and demanded answers. But it is pretty hard to intimidate somebody who is already in Hell. A lot of administrators never learn this, but the Devil had been at it longer than most. So when the old man shrugged again and grinned in his face, the Devil just lit him up one more time and stalked off to find answers for himself.

When the mockingbirds came zooming in the third day, they had a surprise waiting for them.

"Hold it right there!" bellowed the Devil, jumping out from his hiding place behind a rock. Hell was filled with the sound of squeals as the birds hit their air brakes. "Just what do you think you're doing?"

To a bird, those mockers knew exactly what they were doing, but they weren't talking. In fact, with sand in their beaks, they couldn't hardly. The Devil ordered them down, and, while they were hopping from one foot to the other on hot rocks and scorched branches, he gave them a truly administrative chewing out. Flipping through the stone tablets on his clipboard, he hollered about paperwork and deadlines and ended with, "If I catch you all on the property again, each and every one of you is in for a first-degree roasting of your own! Do you understand me?!?"

The mockingbirds understood, all right. They understood that they couldn't help their friend anymore. And that made them sad—about as sad as they felt in the springtime when they couldn't find girlfriends. It made them so sad that they began to sing. One, then two, then a dozen, and pretty soon the whole of Hell was filled with that song. Millions of mockingbirds singing their broken little hearts out. It was beautiful. And Hell was certainly no place for it.

The Devil's eyes bugged out. He told them to stop. He told them to shut up. But anyone who has ever had a sad mockingbird outside his window at three in the morning knows they don't shut up for anything. The Devil fumed and fussed, but, in the end, just like it had gotten to the mean old man, that song got to the Devil. He wound up muttering, digging his cloven toe around in the ashes, and finally blurting out that he couldn't have this sort of thing going on—leads to anarchy— but he didn't suppose there would be any harm in the birds' knowing that he went fishing every Friday. If the old man's bonfire went out on Friday morning, there wouldn't be anyone around to start it back up until Saturday afternoon. That said, the Devil turned on his heel and stomped off.

The mockingbirds looked at their friend. He nodded eagerly. Once a week was better than nothing. Besides, it gave him something to look forward to. In the long run, the tedium in Hell was worse than the heat. This suited the mockingbirds too. They had been neglecting important family matters and they couldn't keep that up forever.

So that is how it all started—why you never see a mockingbird in Florida on a Friday. They all get up early in the morning and fly out to the beaches to get sand. Then they are off to Hell to put out that bonfire and stay for a visit.

This is a true story, but once in a while somebody will see a mockingbird in Florida on a Friday and want to call me a liar. This person is not thinking. Florida is a tourist state. Those are Ohio mockingbirds, down here to visit Disney World.

"I like to tell stories that involve my audience with lots of participation parts in a story. I feel I leave my audiences of all ages—from 3 to 103—knowing they have had an active experience in storytelling that will stay with them."

Linda Morrell Spitzer
Miami

In 1930, Linda Spitzer's grandfather moved his wife, children, brothers, nephews, and cousins to Florida and bought citrus groves in Clermont, where Linda lived until she was six years old. She grew up and went to school in Orlando and now lives in Miami.

For more than thirty years, Linda has been a teacher in Jewish schools as well as a facilitator of workshops in both storytelling and Jewish education for teachers. She earned her master's degree in Storytelling at Eastern Tennessee State University in 1996 and is founder and past president of the Miami Storytellers Guild. She has a regular following for the tales she tells weekly at the historic Biltmore Hotel in Coral Gables. Linda has performed for TV and major storytelling festivals in Miami as well as throughout Florida and in Georgia. She tells her lively tales to all ages as she dramatizes traditional folktales but is best known for her considerable repertoire of Jewish Folktales of Wit and Wisdom and Earth Friendly Tales.

Linda and her husband have three children and eight grandchildren.

The Tale of Rabbit's Tail

A long, long, long time ago, when rabbits used to have long, bushy tails, there was one rabbit who thought he had an exceptionally fine tail. One day he was leaping and bounding down a long, narrow path into the deepest part of the Corkscrew Swamp in Collier County near Ft. Myers. Now this rabbit was small, swift, and tricky. When he came to the end of the narrow path, he stopped because the swamp water was murky—deep red because of the cypress trees and cypress knees in it and muddy because of the alligators in it.

Rabbit was hungry, very hungry, and he had found nothing to suit his taste this blessed morning. But when he looked across that water, he saw something that made his mouth water. On the other side of that swamp there were a number of elderberry bushes covered with clusters of blossoms and a sprinkling of the dark purple berries. And rabbit just lo-o-o-oved elderberry blossoms, and the fruit would be nice for dessert.

"Oh!" he gasped. "Elderberry blossoms and berries! If only I could get to the other side of that muck, I could have myself a feast! But how am I gonna get to the other side?"

Rabbit looked all around for some way to get across the swamp water, for it was a hot day and he was hungry, too hungry and hot to go all the way around.

"I can't swim across or I might be gator meat, and even if I were lucky enough to get across, I'd mess up my fine tail. No, I'll have to think of some other way, but I gotta have some elderberries."

Just then Rabbit got an idea. "Maybe, just maybe, I can get the alligators to take me across on their backs."

So Rabbit hopped up onto a cypress tree stump and shouted at the top of his voice, "Alligator! Alligator! Alligator! Where are you, Alligator?"

Out of that ooshy, gooshy swamp water, a green alligator—all lumpy and bumpy and ug-g-g-ly—poked out his knobby snout. Rabbit smiled and said, "Afternoon, Alligator. How you doin' this fine day?"

"What do you want, Rabbit?" said Alligator.

"Why, Alligator, why do you think there's anything I want? I just came by to see you," said Rabbit.

"I don't want any of your tricks, Rabbit," said Alligator. "I've had enough of your tricks to last me a lifetime."

"Tricks? I got no tricks. It just so happens that I got me a job to do," said Rabbit.

"And what kind of job you got to do?" asked Alligator.

"Well, see, the King of the Swamp has hired me to take a census of all the alligators in this here swamp," said Rabbit.

"Say what?" asked Alligator.

"A census," said Rabbit. "You don't even know what that is, do ya?"

"Yes, I do, but you can remind me," said Alligator.

"Okay," said Rabbit. "A census is when you count everything. I need to count all the alligators in this here swamp, so you need to call all the alligators to come up here so I can count and see how many there are. Then I have to make a report and take it back to the King of the Swamp, who is waiting for me. So you need to be quick and call all your family and friends so I can begin."

Alligator went to the four corners of the swamp calling out "Here, gator, gator. Here, gator, gator!"

And out of that swamp there came dozens and dozens and hundreds and hundreds of alligators—black ones, green ones, and brown ones. They were all lumpy and bumpy and ug-g-g-ly. They looked like a floating bunch of lumpy logs.

"Okay, Rabbit," said Alligator, quite proud of himself for doing such a good job. "I did my part. Now you count all these here alligators."

"Whoo-eee," said Rabbit. "There sure are a lot of alligators. I am impressed." And Rabbit put half of a coconut shell over his right front paw (to impress the alligators that he was an official of the Swamp King) and said, "Now stay where you are." And he started to count. "One, two, three, fo—ohhh. Oh, that alligator just moved and swam under that one over there. And that one over there just went under the water. Let me just start over."

And Rabbit started to count all over again, pointing his shell-covered paw at the alligators. "One, two three, four, fi—hold on there. You can't keep jumping all over each other and swimming. You got to stay still. Alligator, I just can't count them like this. I need you to line 'em up in a straight line from where I'm standing here over to that other side. See? Over there, where that clump of palms is. Otherwise, I can't count 'em. It's up to you, Alligator."

So Alligator yelled at all the alligators, "Line up!" And the alligators all lined up with the nose of one alligator next to the toes of the next alligator, in a straight line from one end of the swamp water to the other. It was a lumpy, bumpy, green-black-brown alligator line.

"There you are, Rabbit. Now start countin' and hurry up!" said Alligator. "We can't stay still like this all day."

So, springing from one alligator's back to the next and tapping each lightly on the head with the coconut shell, Rabbit shouted loudly, "One, two, three." Rabbit jumped on the next alligator's back and said, "Four, five, six, seven."

He jumped with his heart in his mouth onto all those alligators. They all looked at him with their evil, bloodshot eyes but did not attempt to eat him, because they thought Rabbit was on the Swamp King's business.

As he jumped across that alligator line, he continued bumping his coconut shell on the head of every alligator as he counted, without even once getting his tail messed up or his feet wet. Just as he landed on the last alligator's back, Rabbit shouted, "Seven hundred eighty-four. That surely is a lot of alligators."

Rabbit bumped that last alligator's head and was ready to eat those blossoms. But that last alligator was having a bad head day. He wasn't happy about this counting business, even if it was for the Swamp King, and he sure didn't like Rabbit bumping him on the head. So as Rabbit sailed over him, he reached up and bit off most of Rabbit's long, fluffy tail. That's why, to this day, Rabbit has a short, fluffy tail. And that's the end of this rabbit tale.

Ghost Dog of the Biltmore

This tale was inspired by "Black Dog of the Blue Ridge," a folktale retold by Richard and Judy Dockery Young. I have retold it in my own words and have placed it in the Biltmore, where I tell stories every week. People who know of other Biltmore ghost stories say, "Well, I've never heard that one before." Then I tell them, for historical accuracy, that it is based on a folktale.

In the chapter entitled "The Largest Haunted House in America—The Biltmore Hotel" in his book Haunted Houses in America, *Richard Winer writes that parapsychologists agree that ghosts or apparitions haunt places where they met with traumatic experiences during their lives.*

The sky was already turning beautiful purples, pinks, and reds with streaks of brilliant gold. It was twilight at Coral Gables' Biltmore Hotel, and already many people had gathered to see the ghost dog, or, as some folks say, the witch dog. The fifth green of the golf course was bathed in the dappled sunlight, and long shadows were already forming. It was at this time every evening that the huge white dog appeared—walking about two hundred feet onto the fifth green, then turning and walking back and forth, back and forth, like a sentinel on guard, then disappearing at dawn. But let me tell you the story.

In Coral Gables, Florida, there is a majestic, old hotel surrounded by fountains and golf courses and a residential neighborhood. It is called the Biltmore Hotel. It was built in 1926 and has had legends of many ghosts throughout its history. The ghost dog appeared about 1928. At least, that's when the folks of Coral Gables started noticing a huge white dog with long flowing hair. The dog would come out about the same time every evening and then seem to disappear at dawn.

Finally, some young men decided to see if the dog was dangerous and would bother anyone. All of them who had or could borrow horses rode out to the fifth green about the time the dog usually appeared. There he was. They all saw him—a huge white dog, larger than any dog they had ever seen. It walked toward them with a certain dignity. They were curious and prodded their horses to go forward, but when they approached the dog, the horses shied and would go no farther. This they had not expected. So the men had to go back with their questions unanswered.

The next day these young men told everyone who would listen about what they had seen and done. It was decided to go back that night and take guns to kill the dog. They boasted that they would bring back his tail to prove his presence and their success in ridding the place of this apparition. They started at dusk, as they had planned. They were all carrying their guns, but this time, when they got to the fifth green, they hid behind bushes. They were planning an ambush. Just as the last rays of sunlight disappeared from the sky, the big dog was seen taking his usual walk. The men all stood and fired. Every gun was fired, and when the smoke cleared, the great white dog was still walking and pacing, completely ignoring the presence of the hunters. Again and again they fired, and still the dog walked his beat. Can you imagine how frightened the young men were? This was something they had never experienced before, and their hearts were pounding in their chests. Trembling, they ran back to the hotel while the dog continued on his walk, unharmed.

These men told the hotel staff, who told the newspapers, who spread the word about this dog. That's how the story got all around Miami and Coconut Grove and on up to Ft. Lauderdale and even up to the Palm Beach area. That's how the people heard about this ghost dog and came from all over every night to see the great white dog take his walk.

Time passed, and about two years after the dog was first spotted at the Biltmore, a beautiful young woman came to stay at the hotel. Her name was Anna, and she was said to be from Ireland. Reportedly she was trying to locate her husband, who two years before had come to America to find a home for them. When she lost contact with him, she came to America to find him. Anna finally traced him to Coral Gables, and from there all trace of him was lost. Many people she talked to remembered the tall handsome man she described and his dog—a huge white dog with long flowing hair

Then Anna heard the tale of the great white dog that appeared about sunset on the fifth green of the golf course at the Biltmore Hotel, and she pleaded with the people at the hotel.

"You must take me to see this dog. It sounds like it is my husband's dog."

"Lady, you have to understand that the dog could be dangerous. It must be a witch dog, for no one has been able to kill it. We can't let you go near it. Let it be."

"Please," said Anna, "if it's my husband's dog he will know me and no harm will come. Please take me out there tonight."

A party of young men drove her to the golf course in a Model-T Ford. They arrived before dark and Anna got out. She walked over to the fifth green to wait for the dog. As the shadows grew long, the men hid behind the bushes. No one wanted to accompany her out to that lonely fifth green. So she stood out there alone.

As the sun sank, the great dog appeared. When he saw Anna he ran to her and nuzzled his big head into her skirt as she patted him. But then the dog turned and walked a short way, then returned to her, then walked a short way again, looking back at Anna and acting as if he wanted her to follow him.

"It's all right," Anna called out to the men. "I think he wants me to follow him."

Anna followed him over to a large coral rock sitting on the edge of the golf course. The dog began to whine and scratch at the ground below the rock. When Anna got there, he let out a low wail—and then disappeared, vanished.

Anna called out to the men who were watching, "I think he wanted me to dig under the rock. Please, go back and get some shovels. We need to dig under this rock."

Two of the men drove back to the hotel and returned with shovels and flashlights. Some of the men held flashlights while others dug below the rock. They found a shallow grave and in it, the skeleton of a man and the hair and bones of a huge dog. Anna started weeping, and, before they could stop her, she got down into the hole. She bent over and picked up some things and held them up—a ring and a pocket watch.

"These are my husband's," she sobbed. "His initials are on them. Help me remove the bones."

"First, we must call the police."

In due time Anna took the bones of her husband and their dog back to Ireland for proper burial, and the ghost dog of the Biltmore was never seen again.

© 1995 Linda Spitzer

Sandspun

The Peddler of Key West

About threescore years ago, Avrum traveled from Rumania in Eastern Europe to Key West, Florida, where he entered the United States. Avrum earned money to feed his family by being a peddler, that is, by selling things door to door. Avrum wasn't good at this, so the only house he could afford was way out of town. It was a tumbledown shack, and to help feed his family, Avrum grew vegetables in a garden that he planted himself. In the middle of this garden was a large, old Key lime tree.

As I said, Avrum wasn't very good at this peddling work, and sometimes from the sack on his back he gave the stuff away or sold it below cost. When a young boy would come up and ask, "How much for those marbles?" Avrum would say, "That sack of marbles is one quarter." And Avrum would see how sad that little boy was because he knew he didn't have that much money, and then he would say, "Here, you can have them for a nickel."

Or a young girl would come over to see what Avrum was selling and she would see some hair bows she liked. She would pick up a few of those bows and ask, "How much for these hair bows?"

Avrum would say, "Those bows are twenty-five cents each."

When the little girl would say, "Oh, my daddy will never give me money for something like this," Avrum would hand her one bow and say, "Just take one anyway." The girl would say "Thank you" and leave with a smile on her face.

That's how it went, so people used to make fun of the way Avrum did business. They'd say, "He sure doesn't know how to sell things. He just gives everything away."

Avrum had a heart of gold, but too soon he had no gold to buy food for his family, and he had nothing left to sell. Luckily, he still had vegetables growing in the garden, or they would have starved.

One night, Avrum had a dream. In this dream, an old man with long white hair appeared and said, "Go to Miami, to the big hotel with the big tower. See everything that is going on. Hear everything that is going on, and something good will happen for you."

Avrum the peddler woke with a start. He nudged his wife and whispered, "Sarah, wake up. I've had a dream."

Sarah groaned and said, "What?"

"I've had a dream," said Avrum.

"Go back to sleep, Avrum," she said, and she fell asleep again.

Avrum lay awake and wondered about his dream, and after a while he fell asleep. The next night, the old man with the long white hair came again in his dream and said, "Go to Miami, to the hotel with the big tower. Go and be quick. See everything that is going on. Hear everything that is going on, and something good will happen for you."

"Sarah, wake up! Wake up! I've had the same dream again." And Avrum told her about it.

Sarah said, "You would believe anything. Forget about it."

The next morning Avrum told his children about the dream and went about his business. But no matter what he did, he could not get the dream out of his mind. That night, he had the dream again, only the old man with the long hair was more insistent.

"What are you waiting for? Go to Miami, and go to the hotel with the big tower. See everything that is going on. Hear everything that is going on, and something good will happen for you."

The next day Avrum woke up. He was cold and hungry. He could not forget the dream, and when he told Sarah and the children that he had had the dream again, Sarah said, "Perhaps you should go to Miami. Three is a lucky charm."

"I'll go, but I'll be quick about it," said Avrum.

Now it wasn't an easy task to get from Key West to Miami in those days. You had to take a small boat, and it took nearly all day to get there. So the next day, Avrum got up at first light and began to make ready for the journey.

"Tell no one where I've gone because I don't want to be the laughing stock of the town," said Avrum.

Sarah put food, such as they had, into his pack, and a canteen full of water. Avrum kissed his wife and children goodbye. They stood by the door waving, and Avrum walked down to the pier to get on the boat going to Miami. It was a cold day in February with the wind blowing.

During the boat trip, it rained and soaked through his clothes. Water dripped from his nose and he was miserable. By evening the boat reached Miami, and he had eaten up most of his food. It grew dark before he could find shelter, so Avrum had no choice but to sleep out in the open under a tree. When first light came, Avrum tried to get to his feet but found it difficult because of the cramp in his empty stomach and the ache in his body from sleeping outdoors.

He asked the first person he met, "Where is there a hotel with a big tower?"

The stranger said, "Go into Coral Gables. There's a big pink hotel called the Biltmore. You can't miss it."

So after walking for miles and miles and asking many strangers the directions to the Biltmore, Avrum came at last to the big pink hotel with the tower. At the sight of the hotel his heart quickened, and so did his step. There were crowds of people coming and going, men shouting, women jostling and talking, small children laughing, people arriving in cars, and some leaving in auto-gyros, cars with helicopter propellers, for the beach. Avrum had never seen such a sight, and he thanked God that his journey had been safe.

But the moment he arrived at the Biltmore, he started feeling foolish. All his hope and excitement vanished. He really didn't know from his dream what he was supposed to be looking for. So he stood around all day. People passed him this way and that, but no one even looked at him. Having at last found the hotel, he felt utterly lost. He walked up and down, and hour after hour went by. Night came, and again he slept out in the open under a royal poinciana tree. That night he finished the last of his food. He felt foolish, yet what could he do? Again, the next day in front of the Biltmore Hotel, he walked back and forth. He felt lonely, then hopeless. No one took the least notice of the peddler. Tomorrow I'll have to go home; I'm a fool to have come at all, he thought.

The doorman from the hotel walked over to Avrum and said, "What are you doing here? I've been watching you for two days walking in front of the Biltmore from dawn to dusk. You look like you're waiting for a message or directions but no one has talked to you. Why are you here? What are you up to? Who are you waiting for?"

"That's exactly what I was asking myself," said Avrum. "To tell you the truth, I came here because I had a dream that something good would come of it."

"Well," said the doorman, "what a waste of time. I have dreams too, but you don't see me leaving town to chase my dreams. Why, for the last three nights I've had the same dream. In my dream, an old man with long white hair appears and tells me that a chest of gold lies buried under the roots of a Key lime tree in a garden, and that garden belongs to a peddler named Avrum who lives in a tumbledown shack way outside of Key West. Only fools follow dreams. I stay here and attend to my business, which is what you probably should have done. Take my advice and go back home."

"I will," said Avrum, and he thanked the man very much for his advice. The next day, he left Miami on a boat headed back to Key West. Avrum was dirty, aching, and weary but excited. Sarah had never in her life been so glad to see her husband.

"So," asked Sarah, "what of the dream?"

Then Avrum told them all about his journey and his long days outside the Biltmore Hotel, and at last he told them of the doorman's words.

"A man follows a dream and returns with another man's dream," said Sarah. "How strange."

The whole family went outside to the Key lime tree that stood in the garden. Avrum gripped his shovel and began to dig rhythmically. Sweat trickled down his face. All at once, they heard the sound. Avrum took one look at his family and began to dig as fast as he could.

They looked into the hole. "Look, a box!" they cried. They dug the rest of the dirt away with their hands and pulled out a wooden box. It had strange words carved on it. Avrum pulled the top off the box. It was full of gold coins—Spanish gold. Avrum, Sarah, and the children ran their fingers through the gold coins. There were hundreds of them. They took the box inside.

"It's like a dream come true, and because of a dream, we're rich," Avrum said as he sank into a chair.

Avrum was generous with the money. He gave some to the poor and needy, some was given to rebuild a church, some was donated to build a synagogue in town, and the rest of the good things that Avrum did with that money, well, that's another story for another time.

© 1995 Linda Spitzer
storybag@aol.com

"The word delicious means pleasing to the senses. That's what successful storytelling is. The storyteller is dedicated. The storytelling is delicious."

Teresa E. Stein
Lake Placid

A native Floridian and a graduate of Florida State University, Teresa keeps her Florida state teacher's certificate current. She is the owner of a local public relations firm as well as a writer and an adjunct teacher at South Florida Community College.

Teresa wrote the history of Port Everglades for a promotional film in 1959; several historical booklets for South Miami Hospital in the 1960s; the history of the Methodist Church in south Florida in 1975; and an eleven-week series about the history and use of the Florida state park system for the *Tampa Tribune* in 1988. For thirteen years she wrote the Heartland Heritage historical column for the *Tampa Tribune* and for two years broadcast a weekly history radio show, "Florida Cracker Time." Her first published book, *Florida Cracker Tales* Volume 1, now in its fourth printing, was selected by "Talk of the South" for Reading-to-Blind Radio in 1995 and nominated for the Charlton W. Tebeau Award by the Florida Historical Society in 1996. Teresa has also recently published *Florida Cracker Tales* Volume 2, as well as a book about men and women of influence in Florida's history, *Movers and Shakers*.

Teresa has two adopted daughters and two granddaughters.

End's End

If there's one thing that Florida has plenty of, it's snakes! Hunters always keep a wary watch for them, and if you have scrub near your home, it is good advice for you too. I have some woods close to my home, and occasionally I find one curled up on the sun-warmed bricks of my front stoop—just visiting. Even though these are visitors I can do without, snakes are not as bad as their reputation. In fact, they serve a useful purpose in our ecology, and during the Great Depression, a snake gave birth to a new Florida industry.

It was 1926, nearing the end of the Florida real estate boom, when George End, a Connecticut Yankee, moved his family to Arcadia and settled ten miles outside of town in Arcadia Gardens. When the bust came, everyone except the End family left town.

"I think we ought to stay," George told his wife. "It's not gonna be any better anyplace else."

They decided to tough it out, and tough it was. In order to feed his family, George killed every rabbit within walking distance of his home. One day, while hunting on Ninety-Mile Prairie east of Arcadia, George met Guy "Rattlesnake" Johnson, a noted guide for the famed snake handler Ross Allen and for Florida's Pulitzer Prize–winning author Marjorie Kinnan Rawlings. Johnson earned his nickname for his live rattlesnake hunting. He was from Nocatee and hunted the heartland of Florida. He sold his catches to zoos, medical colleges, and vaudeville shows.

George End and Guy Johnson brewed a pot of coffee and sat down to eat their meager lunches. George told Guy of the hardships he and his family were experiencing and asked if he knew of any work.

"Well, I've got orders for a lot of live rattlesnakes. You know, you are livin' right in the middle of the greatest snake-catching territory in the United States. Give it a try. I'll buy all the live snakes you bring to me."

"As bad as I need money, I'm thinkin' that I don't cotton too much to your offer. I'd about as soon starve to death as to be bitten to death by a diamondback."

"If you know what you're doing and keep your mind on your business, there's no reason to ever get bitten. Here, let me show you how."

George End went home feeling good. He had gone out hunting and was not only bringing home a turkey but a job as well. Furthermore, it was a job that his boys could help him with.

After some instruction from their father and a few days of hunting together, the boys were ready to go out on their own. They proudly came home with a six-foot rattler. The only problem was—they had killed him.

"Well, boys," End said when he saw the dead snake, "we can't sell him to Johnson, but let's skin him. Maybe we can sell the hide."

They set to skinning and soon had the job finished. The boys took the skin to prepare it, and George cleaned up the work table. Now hunger will make men do crazy things, and George End was hungry. When he started to throw away the skinned snake, he hesitated. That meat looked so white and nice.

He said to his wife, "Mama, why don't you cook up this purty white meat, and let's see what it tastes like?"

"George End, have you gone loco? Cook and eat a poisonous snake?"

"It's not poisonous. The first thing we did was to get rid of the poison."

Mama cooked it and the family found that it was fine eating! It was so good that they didn't want to let any of it go to waste, so what they couldn't eat they canned.

After this, when End and his boys went snake hunting, they sold the ones they caught alive and cooked the ones they killed. One evening after a special toothsome dish of canned rattlesnake meat, George said, "You know, I believe I could sell it."

But being a former newsman, End knew he could not launch a business in the sparsely populated Florida heartland unless he could get some good advertising, and the only way to get that was with cash or a newsworthy story. When he heard that the Florida Veterans of World War I were going to hold a convention in Tampa, he decided to go and introduce his new product.

He made a friend of the chairman of the committee on eats and drinks and talked him into serving a small portion of snake meat along with the other food at the closing banquet. The meal was served in grand style, and as the diners savored the delicious food, the toastmaster announced that everyone had been served a great delicacy . . . rattlesnake meat!

Some of the audience laughed. Some were angry. Some headed for the door. But the stunt did what End had hoped for. Newspapers from New York to Atlanta and many in between sent reporters for the story.

Immediately the business was a success. End began shipping his canned snake meat all over the United States and Europe. He hired Guy "Rattlesnake" Johnson full-time to catch snakes for his canning plant. Johnson caught more than three thousand for him. End became prosperous and purchased a site at the foot of the Gandy Bridge in Tampa. Opening a store and a snake pit, he petitioned Uncle Sam for a post office license and received it. His new town was named Rattlesnake, Florida.

One day, he was showing a large pet rattler to tourists. For years this snake had been a docile and gentle creature, but this day it bit End on the hand. End, confident that one of his own remedies would work, refused to go to the hospital. When it did not, End was taken to the hospital, but it was too late. End's end came unexpectedly. He died within a few hours.

I don't know, but don't you think that End should have known never to trust the hind end of a mule, the head end of a rattler, or, we might add, a home remedy for a snakebite?

© 1996 Teresa Stein
cracker@digital.net

Index of Names and Places

H

Harry P. Leu Gardens, 79
Hartford, CT, 79, 105
Haunted Houses in America, 128
Healing Arts Group of the
    NSA, 20
"Heartland Heritage," 135
Hell, 121, 122
Hell's Hole, 12
Hendry County In-Service
    Day, 119
Hillsborough County, FL, 79
Ho-bay, 68
Homosassa, FL, 61
Hurricane Andrew, 105
"Hurricane at the Zoo," 105
Hurston, Zora Neal, 78

I

Imagination Factory, 119
Imagine That! Storytellers, 111
India, 24, 41
Indian River, 86
Indiana University, 70
Indonesia, 41
"Infinite Resource and
    Sagacity," 20
Ireland, 129, 130

J

Jacksonville Public Library
    System, 6
Jacksonville, FL, viii, 22
Jamaica, 67

Japan, 45
*Jewish Folk Tales of Wit and
    Wisdom,* 124
Johnson, Col. Robert G., 57,
    58, 59
Johnson, Guy "Rattlesnake,"
    136, 138
Jonathan Dickinson State
    Park, 69
Jones, Charlie, 64
Jumper, Betty Mae, 97
Jupiter, FL, 68, 69
Justice, Jennifer, 46

K

Kaleidoscope Storytellers, 45
Keiser, Henry J., 12
Kentucky, 90
Key West, FL, 131, 134
King of the Crackers, 60
Kirle, Captain Joseph, 66
Kissimmee River, 99, 112
Kissimmee, FL, 35, 37, 40, 99
Ku Klux Klan, 10, 13

L

Lake Okeechobee, 76, 97, 99,
    112
"The Largest Haunted House
    in America – The
    Biltmore Hotel," 128
Leach, Maria, 46
Lebanon, 41
Leesburg, FL, 6

Topical Index

If you enjoyed reading this book, here are some other books from Pineapple Press on related topics. For a complete catalog, write to: Pineapple Press, P.O. Box 3889, Sarasota, FL 34230 or call 1-800-PINEAPL (746-3275). Or visit our website at www.pineapplepress.com.

200 Quick Looks at Florida History by James C. Clark. Covers 10,000 years of Florida history in 200 brief history lessons. A boon to students, newcomers, and those who simply want to learn more about Florida and its rich and varied history, this book is packed with unusual and little-known facts and stories. ISBN 1-56164-200-2 (pb)

Alligator Tales by Kevin M. McCarthy. True and tongue-in-cheek accounts of alligators and the people who have hunted them, been attacked by them, and tried to save them from extinction. Filled with amusing black-and-white photographs and punctuated by a section of full-color photos by award-winning *Gainesville Sun* photographer John Moran. ISBN 1-56164-158-8 (pb)

The Florida Chronicles by Stuart B. McIver. A series offering true-life sagas of the notable and notorious characters throughout history who have given Florida its distinctive flavor. **Volume 1**: *Dreamers, Schemers and Scalawags* ISBN 1-56164-155-3 (pb); **Volume 2**: *Murder in the Tropics* ISBN 1-56164-079-4 (hb); **Volume 3**: *Touched by the Sun* ISBN 1-56164-206-1 (hb)

The Florida Keys by John Viele. The trials and successes of the Keys pioneers are brought to life in this series, which recounts tales of early pioneer life and life at sea. **Volume 1**: *A History of the Pioneers* ISBN 1-56164-101-4 (hb); **Volume 2**: *True Stories of the Perilous Straits* ISBN 1-56164-179-0 (hb); **Volume 3**: The Wreckers ISBN 1-56164-219-3 (hb)

Florida Portrait by Jerrell Shofner. Packed with hundreds of photos, this word-and-picture album traces the history of Florida from the Paleo-Indians to the rampant growth of the late twentieth century. ISBN 1-56164-121-9 (pb)

The Florida Reader: Visions of Paradise edited by Maurice O'Sullivan and Jack Lane. Selections in this collection of stories and essays about Florida range from tales of adventures among Native Americans by the Spanish Gentleman of Elvas to the short stories of Marjorie Kinnan Rawlings, from the romantic reflections of William Bartram and Silvia Sunshine to the carefully crafted prose of Zora Neale Hurston and John Muir. ISBN 1-56164-062-X (pb)

Florida's Past Volumes 1, 2, and 3 by Gene Burnett. Collected essays from Burnett's "Florida's Past" columns in *Florida Trend* magazine, plus some original writings not found elsewhere. Burnett's easygoing style and his sometimes surprising choice of topics make history good reading. **Volume 1** ISBN 1-56164-115-4 (pb); **Volume 2** ISBN 1-56164-139-1 (pb); **Volume 3** ISBN 1-56164-117-0 (pb)

Forever Island and *Allapattah* by Patrick Smith. *Forever Island* has been called the classic novel of the Everglades. *Allapattah* is the story of a young Seminole in despair in the white man's world. ISBN 0-910923-42-6 (hb)

Legends of the Seminoles by Betty Mae Jumper. This collection of rich spoken tales—written down for the first time—impart valuable lessons about living in harmony with nature and about why the world is the way it is. Each story is illustrated with an original painting by Guy LaBree. ISBN 1-56164-033-6 (hb); ISBN 1-56164-040-9 (pb)

Southeast Florida Pioneers by William McGoun. Meet the pioneers of the Palm Beach area, the Treasure Coast, and Lake Okeechobee in this collection of well-told, fact-filled stories from the 1690s to the 1990s. ISBN 1-56164-157-X (hb)

Tellable Cracker Tales collected by Annette Bruce. Memorable characters from Florida history come alive in these folktales and legends, tall tales, and gator tales. Pull up your favorite chair and a few listeners and start your own storytelling tradition with the gems in this collection. ISBN 1-56164-100-6 (hb); ISBN 1-56164-094-8 (pb)